Dawn's Renaissance

Dawn's Renaissance

By T.C. Florer

Published by Timothy C. Florer
Copyrights by Tim Florer
Diana Willits Project Director
Designed by Leng Vong Reiff, Akili Design & Marketing Services, Inc.

First edition October 2014, proudly printed by
ISBN: 9780692302255

Author's Note

So many of you have asked, " What happened to Dawn after Chet died? How did she get through the grief ? What did she do with the rest of her life? Did she find someone else, or is she still alone?"

I was like all of you. I wanted, no, I needed to follow the story.

Their lives had somehow intertwined with mine, and Dawn was gracious over the following years, allowing time for me. We would meet in the cabin on Black Duck, and I would listen. She would tell me memories that just seemed to flow from her heart.

Sometimes, we would gather up one dozen chocolate chip cookies and a thermos of coffee, and take *AUTHOR* for a ride up to the falls. We would sit quietly and watch the bald eagles swoop down from the trees to catch a walleye for lunch. Dawn would always say, " This was Chet's favorite spot. He relished the sounds of the water and wind, the absolute sacred feeling of being a part of Creation."

We had other meetings at the farm off the two-lane road in Story County, Iowa. On more than one occasion, Dawn permitted me to mow the homestead with Chet's John Deere tractor, with one specific instruction. " Do not mow in the pine grove. I do that with an old push reel mower. Chet always loved the sound the reel made as the clippings flew in the air and landed on his feet. He said that was his personal contribution to the Green Revolution."

We would always end these meetings at the farm in the same way. It was like a religious experience. Dawn would always make ham and cheese sandwiches, topped off with lettuce from her garden, with red radishes on the side, and serve large glasses of iced tea. We would eat at the bistro table in the screened-in porch, and desert was always the same. Dawn called it, " Better than Sex" cake. She would always smile while eating desert, while a far-away look came across her eyes.

After dinner, without fail, she would walk me to my car, give me a hug, and start to hum the song,

Faded Photographs.

Her blessings for this manuscript came with two simple rules: I was never allowed to use her real name, and I had to tell it truthfully, wherever it would lead.

Dawn's other request was simple. I was to start this story with the end of the poem she had written for Chet before he died.

And so I shall.

To receive all that is given
And return more
So when you leave, I forever will have
Your saving
Grace

T. C. Florer

Dedication

To my grandchildren: Wren, Harlan, Everett, and Reilly Rose.
You represent the future of our family, and I love you dearly.
It is an honor to be called "Popa"!
I trust you will carry on the tradition of the
"unexpected kindness".

Chapter 1

A butterfly came to rest on the nape of Dawn's neck, and fluttered ever so lightly.

And she knew.

At that same moment, a loon surfaces next to the boathouse and sounds its haunting call.

Dawn bows her head, wipes the tears from her eyes, and clasps her hands together and whispers, " He is yours now. I pray that you will watch over him, give him peace, and remind him I will join him someday. Amen."

She gathers her composure and goes back inside the cabin to phone the Norseman Gallery. Karen answers, and Dawn asks, "Will you and Chuck please go to the farm and check on Chet? In my heart, I can feel he is gone." Karen replies, " We will leave right now, and will call you in twenty minutes."

They arrive and look inside the house. On the kitchen table, resting against the salt and pepper shakers, is a thick envelope addressed to *My, Lover Dawn*. They search the rest of the house, then the office building, then the machine shed. No trace of Chet. They both look at each other, then walk down to the pine grove.

Chet is found sitting in his Adirondack chair. Each of his arms is resting on the wide chair arms, with a copy of his first book under his right elbow, and both of his hands are in a palms up position — as if he was going to receive communion.

Chuck whispers, " Look how peaceful his smile is." Karen touches Chet lightly on his forehead and says, " He is already cold. We have to call Dawn back." As she dials, Chuck takes off his jacket and covers Chet's face and upper body. Dawn answers on the first ring, and Karen, in a choked-up voice, says, " He went peacefully."

Chapter 2

Dawn steels herself to prepare for all the arrangements that must be made. She tells Karen, " Please call the funeral home in Story City. They will take care of Chet, he left them instructions six months ago." Karen replies, " Consider it done. Dawn, when we went inside the house, we noticed an envelope on the kitchen table addressed to *My Lover, Dawn*." Dawn could sense the sadness in Karen's voice, and said, " Please leave it where it sits. I am leaving now, and should be there in seven hours. Thank you, both of you, for being there for him."

Seven hours to think of all that had to be decided. Dawn said aloud to herself in the car, " Knowing him, that envelope will contain everything I will need to know, that all the tough decisions have been made, to take the burden off of my soul. I would expect nothing less from Chet. I'll spend this time remembering us."

As she headed south on the 456-mile trip to be with him, Dawn's memories came together to play out their twenty-year love affair, as if it had started just yesterday.

That day in June, 1990, on the Terrace of the Memorial Union at Iowa State University, where the reception was held for the writer's workshop attendees. Chet was the benefactor and the instructor, pledging to sponsor the next wave of storytellers. When his eyes met hers, Dawn remembered, " It was as if he was looking inside me, my heart, my brain, my soul, his eyes searching for an answer, and I had no idea what the question was." How, by the end of the workshop, she knew the answer, and had fallen in love with him, the man she had prayed for all her adult life.

She thought of the black and white calendar, and how she had crossed off thirty days in a row, and on that last day, they had become lovers. On the twenty-ninth day, Chet had given her a hand-bound book of poems he had written, printed on velum.

She ran the titles through her mind, *Sweep the Floor Clean, Abandoned Homestead, Whisper, Spring,* and

Her Irresistible Neck. As she continued the drive south, she recited each poem, word for word, and remembered the internal glow she felt the first night she had read them.

Glancing at her engagement ring, a rose-cut diamond surrounded by four emeralds, she remembered how he had proposed at the art gallery, and how she had said, " Yes, and what took you so long!"

By the time Dawn crossed the Minnesota and Iowa border, her tears were flowing freely. The years were playing in her mind, and the common theme was how deep their love was, a love full with mutual respect, quiet conversation, supporting each other's endeavors, romantic and fulfilling love making, and butterfly kisses.

With a painful ache in her heart, she thought, " We were so blessed to have a total relationship. There are couples who have been married for fifty-plus years that have never reached the inner peace that we possessed."

Chapter 3

Dawn arrived at the farm, off the two lane road, after sunset. She went inside the house, turned on the lights, and saw the envelope addressed to her on the kitchen table. After starting a pot of coffee, she went to the bedroom closet and pulled out one of Chet's flannel shirts and put it on. Just smelling his scent seemed to comfort her.

She sat at the table with a fresh cup of coffee and picked up the envelope. Running her fingers over it, she imagined him sealing the envelope with a feeling of relief, as if it was one more detail that he could finish for her. Just seeing the word, *Lover,* on the outside warmed her deepest core. She opened it, and found several different letters.

The cover letter read:

My Dearest Dawn,

I have tried to plan ahead for this moment. The first letter explains my funeral arrangements, the second is about my estate, and the third is a poem to you that I wrote while I was still lucid. As you go through all of this in the next few days, just remember that I am here, for you. Just close your eyes, think of me, and I will be there.

With eternal love,
Chet

After taking a sip of coffee, Dawn unfolded the letter titled:

Funeral arrangements

I have been given permission from the ISU Provost to have my visitation held in the Gold Star Hall in the Memorial Union. It is such a hallowed place, and some of my paramount life moments happened around this space.

Dawn, I especially like the quote that is above the west entrance from M.J. Riggs, ISU class of 1883: " We come to college not alone to prepare to make a living, but to learn to live a life."

After visitation, my casket is to be moved to the Memorial Chapel. Pastor Nilsen has agreed to perform the service; he officiated at Michelle's funeral. There will be communion offered to all at the rail, and Dawn, you may decide who gives the eulogy, if any.

My music choices are, " Jesus Loves Me, Yes I Know" and my favorite Tony Bennett song, " I'll Be Seeing You".

After the service, a lunch will be served at the Union Café. Just contact the events manager at 294-1437, and he will make sure everything proceeds as planned, and I have already paid for it. Please make sure that any left-over food is sent to the mission on Main Street.

The following day, my casket should be taken to Black Duck, and burial will be next to Michelle. Dawn, I pray that you will be laid to rest next to me, but not for decades. Pastor Hutton, who married you and me, has offered to perform the graveside service.

My tombstone will come from Monuments Inc. in Virginia, Minnesota. It is white marble with black lettering.

Chester T. Carrington
1952-
Husband to Michelle Bastien
Then
Husband to Dawn Wilson
He touched people with words

Dawn, these are my wishes. If you are uncomfortable with any of these requests, I trust that you will make the decisions that you can live with.

Eternally yours,
Chet

Dawn reviewed the letter, and was so thankful that Chet had foreseen what was needed, and, after filling her cup again with coffee, decided that she would not change any of his requests.

Sitting back down at the table, Dawn unfolded the letter about his estate:

My dearest,

I hired a law firm in Ames last year to begin the process of protecting my estate for you. The firm is Dewey, Cheetum, & Howe, and their office is on Duff Street.

The farm, the cabin, and all personal possessions go to you. Life insurance will provide $600,000.

My SEP will pay you $2,000 per month for the rest of your life.

All the royalties from my books will be paid to you. A monthly check will be sent from THE WRITTEN WORD.

I have set up a trust fund that will provide a writer's workshop each year at ISU. There are enough funds to pay expenses for 20 attendees and the fee and expenses for a speaker. You have been named the sole trustee for this.

I have also set aside bank CD's for an idea I would like you to develop. You could set up a writer's camp at the farm for 5 children to attend each summer. You could show them how much power is in the written word, how they can use their imagination to express their feelings and emotion. Dawn, you could teach them self-worth and confidence. I think your mother, Kris, would be thrilled, since that is what she did for all her piano students.

There are other minor details that you can work out with the lawyers. I hope this takes some burden from your shoulders.

I will miss your scent,
Chet

Dawn set those two letters aside, uttering a prayer thanking Chet for planning so she could live the rest of her life in financial comfort. They never talked about it, but knowing him, she was always comfortable in the fact that he would make sure she would be taken care of financially, after he was gone. She had done the same for him with her TSA, pension, and insurance.

She returned her coffee cup to the counter, and poured a large glass of merlot. She was ready to read the most important of the letters, since it would come straight from Chet's heart. She sat back down, took a long drink of wine, opened up the poem, and began to cry as she read the title.

My Dawn

Blessed I am to have loved

To those who say, "Love at first sight"
I reply, "It happened to me twice"
First
As a young man
Full of inexperience and expectations
As was she
Her first time, not mine
Coming together as one
Physically and emotionally
To start off with unspoken rules
Listen, not only with ears, but also with eyes
See, not only with eyes, but also with heart
To touch, and know when not to
To wrap up in embrace, to know when to give space
To support their idea, even if you disagree
And receive the same in return
To not touch, and still feel the pulse
To not speak, and still hear the words
Year after year

Deeper, fuller, richer
Like chocolate and wine
Life had become a dessert
That was taken away
By
Death

I
Wandered
For five years
In the wilderness of life
Like an animal who licks his wounds
Wary of surroundings
Healing
But leaving scars
Using others for pleasure
Then discard
Erecting a shield to prevent anyone from taking
Or was it to protect from receiving
And then came you
On that afternoon in June
I shook your hand and looked into your eyes
As you said your name
" I am Dawn"
I thought, " First light before sunrise"
This beauty in the black dress
Will be my light

For the rest of my life
Looking into your soul
I asked the question without speaking
And in three days you answered
Those blue eyes seeking
"Yes!"
We grew together as one
Each bringing puzzle pieces
That fit to become
A stunning original portrait
Of unlimited love
We each followed our own path
Without
Loosing sight of each other
You became my Muse
From all my emotions sprang words and thoughts
That became books and poetry
In hopes of touching at least one life
And you said, " You have touched mine."

Dawn
You healed all my wounds and vanished my scars
So I could find a depth of love
Never before imagined
Bless you for taking all you could
Bless you for returning more
I am a better person

Because of you
As I close my eyes for that final time
As I shed those final tears
Know my lover
My last thought
Was
Of
You

Chet Carrington

Dawn laid the letter — soaked by her tears — down on the table, and began to sob, the release of her pain racking her body. She knew the void in her soul would never be as deep as it was in this moment. The finality of never again seeing him in the morning, hearing his voice, feeling his touch, the exhalation he brought to her when he explored her body, and the loving look in his eyes when he gazed at her. It was all gone, but to survive, she knew she had to lean on the memories they made together.

And God knows, what memories she had. From the first time they met, to the last time she kissed him, their life was filled with those precious moments that others only dream about, a fairy tale, lived out daily. There were enough, she felt, to pull her through this dark time, and she could become a stronger person in the end.

She picked the letter up again, and held it to her heart, knowing that these few pages were his masterpiece, full of real emotion, and some mystery. Chet had never spoken about the five years between the death of Michelle, and the day in June 1990, when they met, except for a mention of how cold and rainy it was in Portland in the winter. She realized those secrets were gone forever.

Dawn regained some composure, poured another glass of merlot, and stepped outside. The moon was full now, just as it was the night Chet had given her a single red rose with a card that simply said, *As One.* She needed to walk to the pine grove and sit in his chair, to feel the wood as he had felt it, to catch the fragrance of the pines that had been refreshed by the evening dew, and catch a gentle breeze that would make that magical sound through the pine boughs that he so cherished.

She tilted her head back as she took a sip of wine, and in the north sky, a single falling star lit up the sky. Dawn raised her glass as if giving a toast and said, " To you, my lover and best friend, one day we will be together again.

Chapter 4

As Dawn began walking back to her house, a pair of headlights came up the driveway. She heard the car stop, and saw her old friend, Audry Chance, step out. With a feeling of relief, Dawn ran to greet her. As they embraced, Audry whispered in her ear, "Honey, I was there to help you when your mom passed, and I am here now to help you through this. Now, let's go inside before we freeze our, you know, off." Dawn laughed for the first time that day as she and Audry went into the house. Audry had an overnight bag that she put on the couch, and as she pulled out a bottle of *Templeton Rye* whisky, she said, "I'll take the couch tonight, and I brought this whisky for medicinal purposes. You need a drink, and I sure as hell wouldn't be a good guest if I didn't join you. I'll grab the glasses if you'll get some ice."

With full glasses, they sat at the dining table, and Dawn asked, with a quizzical look, " How did you know that Chet was gone?" Audry replied, "Honey, Chet told the funeral home director to call me as soon as it happened. He wanted me to be here for you.

There are a few things you don't know about your husband, and it's time to fill you in. Right after you two tied the knot, I ran into him at the Campus Book Store. We went downstairs to have a coffee, and I looked him square in the eye and told him that if he didn't treat you like a princess I would be on him like flies on, you know. He laughed so hard, I thought he would pass out, and told me that you would be treated like royalty. I told him, "O.K., enough said!"

Dawn, from then on, he would phone me every two weeks, and the first words he would say were, "Audry, how are you?" He would listen as I talked about any ailments I had, my rants against the damn politicians, and when, in season, ISU basketball. And every phone call ended with him offering, "Audry, if you need anything, call me." There were times that I asked him to find me a ninety-year-old millionaire who needed a companion, but that never happened! Honey, those phone calls meant a lot to me, and it showed what a caring person he was. I won't be surprised if, in the next month or so, that people will come up to you and tell you how Chet helped them out. And the great thing about it was how humble he was, never making a big deal over it. He would tell me, "It's what we are suppose to do. It's that simple." Audry drained her glass, and got a refill, while Dawn nursed her first one.

They began to remember how they met years ago, how Audry had taken Dawn under her wing in her first teaching job. They both shed a tear when they talked about Dawn's mother, Kris, and the escapades they all had together in Burlington each summer. Audry said, "Remember your mom and I asking, "Frog or Prince" when you came home from playing piano at that joint, what the hell was the name of it?" Dawn laughed, and replied, "Yes I remember, and only one time did I say Prince, the night I met Brent Makenzie. And the name of the joint was Don't Muddy the Waters."

They talked till midnight, when Audry said, "I think it's time to hit the sack, God knows I need all the beauty sleep I can get! We can deal with reality in the morning." Dawn kissed her on the forehead, and quietly said, "Thank you"

And as Dawn fell asleep, holding Chet's pillow to her breast. She thought in silence, "Chet, thank you for sending Audry to me, tonight. I love you."

Chapter 5

The following morning, Dawn was awakened by the delicious scents of eggs, bacon, and coffee that had wafted into her bedroom. She thought, "That was so nice of Chet to fix breakfast!", then realized it couldn't be him, and she knew this would be just the first of many moments that would be in the zone between fantasy and reality.

She threw on one of his flannel shirts and found Audry sitting at the table, reading the morning paper. She looked up at Dawn and said," I thought you were going to sleep all day, and I would be forced to eat a pound of bacon by myself. Pull up a chair and I will fix your plate. Coffee?" Dawn nodded in reply, and thought of how blessed she was to have this good of a friend.

They ate in silence, and after Audry cleared the table, she asked, "O.K., what do you have to do today?" Dawn told her that she needed to call the newspapers to place an obituary. Audry replied, "Give me the names of the papers, and I will find their numbers. I would guess they are the *AMES TRIBUNE, IOWA STATE DAILY,* and *THE DES MOINES REGISTER.*" Dawn added, "There is a weekly that covers Black Duck Lake, I think it's called *NORTHERN WOODS JOURNAL.*"

Audry found all the numbers, and Dawn began to call. Each paper routed her call to the senior editor, and they all expressed their condolences to Dawn. And if she would give them the information, they all offered to write the obit personally. She thanked them, and proceeded with the facts:

Chester T. Carrington of rural Story City, Iowa and Black Duck, Minnesota, passed away peacefully yesterday. Born in 1952, he was the only child of Frank and Mary Carrington. He received his B.A. from ISU in 1974, and his Masters in 1976, also at ISU. Chet was a successful author who had five books on the New York Times Bestseller list. He also was the founder of a writer's workshop at ISU. He always shunned the limelight, and protected his privacy.

His parents and his first wife, Michelle Bastien, preceded him in death. His wife, Dawn, is his sole survivor. Mr. Carrington requested that no flowers be sent, that all contributions be given to the Story County Alzheimer's Association.

Visitation will be this Friday, 10:00 A.M., at the Gold Star Hall on the ISU campus, followed by a short service in the Memorial Chapel. Burial will be a private affair.

With the first of many decisions completed, Audry said, "That's enough for today. Let's jump in the car, drive on the two lane, and find a piece of pie. Remember your mom's answer to the question, "What is your favorite pie?" Dawn laughed and said with mock authority, "Hot or cold!"

They cleaned up and headed out, the silence in the car comforting to Dawn, and they found a great apple crumb pie in the restaurant at the Boondocks.

When they arrived back home, the sun was setting, and Audry took Dawn's hands and said, " I need to go home now. If there is anything I can help with, just call. I will be there for you Friday morning. One suggestion, when it gets bad, and it will, this pain you have, write him a letter. It just might help. Remember, I love you like a daughter. Enough said."

Audry kissed Dawn on the forehead, then left in her car. What was left was silence.

Chapter 6

For Dawn, the next few days were spent in an emotional state of fog. From sunrise to sunset, her eyes saw all the things in her surroundings that was their history.

From his office, the computer that had turned out book after book, the black and white images he had purchased that inspired his poems, *Sweep the Floor Clean* and *Abandoned Homestead,* an entire bookcase filled with three-ringed binders that held all his original notes and background information, and his Montblanc pen resting on a fresh legal pad, as if it were waiting for Chet's hand to pick it up and begin another best seller.

Inside the house, Dawn found comfort in being enveloped in all that was there, his favorite chair, electric shaver, coffee mug, a collection of ISU hats, and his cuff links and matching ring. He had commissioned Brooke, of b. shannon designs in Winterset, to make them. Dawn thought that is was a shame that Chet had no heir to pass these on to, but life is what it is.

Chuck, Karen, and Lou would either call or drop by to offer quiet support, and Dawn had long conversations with Sondra Whitman, Chet's publisher at *The Written Word.* His passing had gone viral on the internet, and their office had been flooded with e-mails of condolence and a huge up-swing in orders for all his books. She assured Dawn that she, along with the Conners, would fly in on Thursday to attend the service on Friday.

On Friday morning, Dawn drove to the ISU campus and parked in the Union ramp. She arrived an hour early so she could spend some private time with Chet. She thought that he looked peaceful, and his hands were holding his Bible, the one he received in 1961 from Pastor Miene for learning all the books in the Bible, in order.

Dawn had brought the stool from home to sit on, the one that Chet had used twenty years ago at Morrill Hall when he told the story of Michelle Bastien and Jim Smith at the writer's workshop.

By 10:00 A.M., the line of visitors stretched from the Gold Star Hall to the Campanile. The majority were students who were, in some way, touched by Chet's writings. Some quietly told Dawn that reading his works helped them to decide to pick English and Composition as their field of study. Dawn felt warmed that he had accomplished this, and knew he would never take any credit.

When the bells struck at noon, Chet's casket was moved into the chapel, where Pastor Nilsen gave a heartfelt service. There was not a dry eye in the room.

Afterwords, a lunch was held at the Union Café, where Dawn said her goodbyes, and retrieved her car for the long drive to Black Duck. She had requested that she and Pastor Hutton would be the only ones in attendance at the gravesite. Audry had volunteered to go with her, but Dawn gently told her this is what she wanted, and Audry had smiled at her and commented, "Enough said."

Dawn followed the hearse to Black Duck, remembering on the long drive all the times she had come here with Chet. The love they shared here was more than most people could fathom. It was pure, unselfish, all-encompassing. She thought of how blessed she was to have the time she did with him.

They arrived at the burial site on the knoll above the cabin at eight that evening. There was just enough light to have the service. Pastor Hutton said, "Ashes to ashes, dust to dust", Dawn laid one perfect red rose on the casket and whispered, "As one."

She asked the Pastor to give her a minute, and as he stepped back, she knelt down on the grave of Michelle, and with tears running down her face, her heart broken, she choked out these words, "Michelle, I am returning him to you for now. Know that he always carried his love for you in his heart, and I always respected that. I feel he communicated with you in these last years, and I know he will be safe with you, and in God's hands. Someday, I will join both of you."

Dawn struggled to regain some degree of composure, and joined the Pastor as the funeral crew closed up the grave.

After a final look, she and Pastor Hutton walked down the knoll to the cabin where he said to her, "Peace be with you" then he took his leave. Dawn went inside, poured a glass of merlot, and after taking a sip, set the challis on top of the piano. She began to caress the keys as she sang the song she had written for him, the refrain being *To receive all that is given and return more, so when you leave, I forever will have your saving grace.*

Chapter 7

Pity will only go so far in healing a person's soul, and by the following Friday, Dawn had realized that she had used her share. The emptiness and ache would be there for months, maybe even years. She knew it was time to start the next stage of her life, and that was to fulfill Chet's final wishes.

With a view of the lake outside her living room window, Dawn sat at the table and took out a legal pad and began to write down a list of decisions:

1. *Leave everything in place here at the lake. No need to give his clothes away yet. I have room, and they help comfort me.*
2. *Same decision about the farm. Leave it as he left it.*
3. *Meet with the attorneys to discuss the Chester T. Carrington Memorial Writer's Workshop for June of next year.*
4. *Contact ISU Provost to secure the same lecture hall where it all started. Get contact information for the Union to reserve a block of 21 rooms for the workshop participants, including the guest instructor.*
5. *Contact Sondra Whitman at the Written Word to see whom she would recommend for the instructor.*
6. *Procure a list from Amazon.com of the top twenty self-published authors. They would comprise the first class.*
7. *Contact Story County Human Services Department to inquire about local foster children. Explain the concept of a writer's workshop for children. Check to see if permits or licenses are required. Plan to start the third week of August this year.*

Dawn laid down her pen and read the list over, again. To herself, she said, " That should keep me engaged."

She went to the kitchen and made a ham and cheese sandwich with home-grown lettuce, grabbed some radishes and a bottle of iced tea, and placed it all in a cooler. With a bag of chocolate chip cookies and the cooler in hand, Dawn went to the boathouse and untied the mooring ropes on *Author,* and headed to the falls.

When she arrived, she ate her lunch, her soul wrapped in the sounds and the beauty of the spot that Chet so loved. She vowed that she would complete all his wishes, and the return would be that someone's life would be touched, and that was the essence of Chet.

After lunch, she went back to the cabin to make the phone calls that would begin her quest.

The first call was to the Provost at ISU. Dawn thanked him for all the arrangements he made for Chet's service, and he said, "You are more than welcome, but it is, I, who should be thanking you. Chet left $50,000 to Morrill Hall. With that money, we have named the lecture hall where he conducted his first workshop the Chester T. Carrington Memorial Hall. We at the University guarantee that each June, that hall will be available to you for a workshop for as long as you wish."

Dawn thanked him, and informed him that indeed, there would be a workshop next June. When she hung up the phone, she smiled at the thought of Chet taking care of things before he passed, yet again showing why he was so easy to love.

Her next call was to the Memorial Union. Within 15 minutes she had locked in a block of rooms for the 21 participants, and had decided on all the food menus.

Dawn then contacted the attorney's office, brought them up to speed, then made a pot of coffee.

With a full cup in hand, she then called Sondra at *The Written Word* to discuss potential guest instructors. Sondra inquired about how Dawn was holding up, and Dawn replied, " Keeping busy really helps, I think that was part of Chet's plan. I am hosting a writer's workshop next June, all the plans have been made. Would you please help me by picking a guest instructor who is now just emerging on the national scene? I trust your judgment, and I would like to have the selection firmed up by October 1st." Sondra assured her she would make this favor top priority, and would call Dawn back as soon as possible.

After finishing the call to Sondra, she decided that she would drive back to the farm in the morning, and begin to tackle the foster child program. That left her the rest of the afternoon and evening to play piano and remember him.

Chapter 8

Before she left the next morning, she called Harry and Alice Hanson to tell them she would be gone for at least a month, and asked them if they would watch over the cabin. They assured her they would take care of it as if it were their own. She thanked them, and then loaded up her car for the drive back home.

Dawn spent the time driving thinking and planning the foster child program that Chet had suggested. She decided that the first class should be comprised of three teenagers to establish a base line of how the program would eventually be structured.

She would develop a flexible idea of what she wanted to accomplish, and thought that Audry would be a great sounding board. She decided to call her the next day to invite her to lunch at Hickory Park.

When she arrived at the farm, she opened the living room windows to let in fresh air, made a pot of coffee, and with a fresh cup in hand, began to make her phone calls.

The first call went to Story County Human Services. She talked with Jenny Black, who, years ago, taught school with Dawn in Story City. Jenny said, with excitement, "I have been waiting for your call. The rumor mill has been going full-tilt, and if what I hear is true, I have three girls, sisters, who would be great for your program!"

Dawn laughed for the first time in weeks, and replied, "I had forgotten how folks in small towns rally around. Let me explain how this will be structured. The students, during the summer, will spend Monday and Friday with me at the farm from 9:00 A.M. till 3:00 P.M. Once school starts, I would want them every other Saturday, at the same time slot. We would work on writing skills, develop their confidence, and encourage an expansion of their imagination. There would be no cost to the students, the foster parents or the county. Jenny, how does all that sound?"

Jenny proclaimed, "Great! I have already cleared this with the Board of Supervisors and there will be no red tape. Now, let me tell you about the girls. Wren is 14, has red hair, and has an old soul. Meadow is 13, has strawberry blonde hair, and has a need to please. Finally, there is Lark, age 12, blonde hair, and lives up to the definition of her name in the dictionary, to engage in harmless fun or mischief."

"Their story is very sad. Two winters ago, up on Highway 20, a semi crossed over the centerline and hit the Russell's car head-on. Both of the girl's parents were killed instantly. Thank God the girls were spending the night with their only grandparent, Sadie Russell. Dawn, she is the foster parent, in her late 70's, and needs help. She is a wonderful woman, but I don't think God gave us enough energy to keep up with three teenaged girls."

"Sadie wants to have you over for Sunday dinner at noon. Will that work for you?" Dawn replied, "Yes, firm it up with Sadie, and e-mail me the address and phone number. And Jenny, thank you."

Chapter 9

Dawn had a nice phone conversation with Sadie on Saturday, and she had requested that Dawn arrive at 11:00 A.M. on Sunday to see how the three girls worked together preparing dinner.

Their home was four miles southwest of Story City. The house was an old style, two-story, four-square, with a screened in porch that wrapped around the whole house. The house sat in the exact middle of 640 acres, prime Iowa land, that Sadie's grandparents had settled on in the late 1800's. Sadie and her husband, Sam, had converted the farming operation to complete row crop, and all of the original out buildings, along with the grove of trees that protected the north side of the house, and fences, had been destroyed. The only newer building was a metal machine shed that housed all of the farm machinery.

Upon arriving, Dawn entered the front porch and knocked on the door. Sadie greeted her, and led her into the parlor. She then called out to the girls, " Girls. Come meet Mrs. Carrington."

Wren, Meadow, and Lark introduced themselves, and Dawn said, " Please, from now on, call me Dawn. Now, can I help you three with dinner?" They motioned her into the kitchen where Sadie sat at the table and Dawn stood next to the sink and watched the three girls in awe. They were like a top-flight surgical team, with Wren clearly in charge. There was no wasted motion as they prepared a dinner of ham, baked potatoes, green beans, and a steaming apple pie that Meadow had just pulled from the oven.

Lark was in charge of setting the table, Meadow gave drink options of iced tea or milk, and Wren brought all the platters of food to the table. Sadie said Grace, and the room grew quiet as everyone dug in to the farm-style meal.

Halfway through dinner, Dawn, after complimenting the girls on an excellent feast, asked the girls what were their favorite subjects in school. Wren answered history, Meadow mentioned writing, and Lark chirped that hers was art. That information helped solidify the idea in Dawn's mind for the first assignment.

After the girls cleared the table, and Sadie served the apple pie, Dawn began to explain her concept, "I have a subject that might interest all three of you. In 1935, there was a great sculpture that arrived at ISU. His name was Christian Petersen, and he became an artist in residence on campus from 1935 to 1961. He taught many students the art of sculpture, and made many pieces that are spread across campus, even now. Some of the most famous are , "The Gentle Doctor", "Four Seasons Fountain", "Conversations", and "Boy and Girl". With Sadie's permission, I would like to take you three on an all day field trip to ISU, and we will visit each sculpture, taking our time to watch the light move over them, touching them to get the feel for each piece. Then I would ask that each of you think for a few days what you saw, how you felt, what they meant to you, and then write a piece about them. And, we will also eat lunch at the Memorial Café, my treat. So, what do you think?"

Wren asked Sadie if it was all right with her, Meadow asked if she could bring her camera, and Lark's concern was if the Café served malts!

With a smile, Dawn announced, "O.K., it looks like we have an adventure to go on. Sadie, may I pick up the girls on Friday morning at 9, and I will have them home by 3?" Sadie agreed, and Dawn told the girls "goodbye." She got into her car and started the drive home feeling good inside. She knew she had an opportunity to make a difference in all of their lives, including hers.

Chapter 10

The following morning, Dawn called Audry to confirm their lunch date at Hickory Park at noon, and Audry proclaimed, "Well, hell yes I remember we are eating together today. I even skipped the slop they call breakfast here at Che Villa. See you at high noon." And then she hung up. Dawn always got a laugh from her talks with Audry, short, to the point, then gone.

Dawn spent the rest of the morning opening another stack of mail. Each week, after his death, cards of condolence and checks to the charity continued to flow in, and Dawn took the time to write a personal thank you to each one. The next letter she opened really surprised her. It was from Brent Makenzie.

To Dawn,

I read about Chet's passing in the Des Moines Register. You have my deepest condolences. You know, from my past, that I have an idea of what you are going through. I suggest that you remember as many of the good memories you and Chet had together, and cherish them deeply. The void in your heart will heal slowly, but remember, you two had something that will never be lost, and that is true love.

If you ever need to talk, I am still a world champion at listening. I would love to hear your voice.

Peace be with you,
Brent

Dawn then noticed a check in the envelope made out to the Story County Alzheimer's Unit for $1,000 dollars. She thought, "How nice of him to write, and what a generous donation." And she recalled those words that ended the poem he had written so many, many years ago, "*Years from now, a warm memory, turns into a smile, when I remember you,*" and indeed, Dawn did smile. She wrote down his phone number from his check, and placed it in her desk drawer. In the back of her mind, she knew, she would call him someday.

After finishing her correspondence, she noticed it was time to leave to meet Audry. As she drove, she remembered going to Brent's opening at the gallery, and the black and white images of the Mississippi River region. She physically shook her head as if to shake those thoughts out of her mind, hoping they would pass, it was still Chet's time.

She arrived at Hickory Park a few minutes late, and found Audry at a table, whose first words were, "Girl, you might be a little late, and at my mature age, I don't have time to waste, so let's order!" Dawn apologized, they ordered, and she began to fill Audry in on the new developments with the three girls.

After she had explained the Christian Petersen angle, Audry told her, "First thing, I think it is great that you are doing this, what a way to honor Chet's wishes; second thing, I agree that kids today need to be exposed to the art that is around them, to see and feel it, physically. It is a way to get them up off their butts, and their heads out of all the computer crap that surrounds all of us. You know, when I started teaching, each student had a Big Chief writing tablet and a #2 pencil. Now, each kid has an electronic notepad connected to the Internet, and instead of face-to-face conversations, they text each other, even when they are in the same room. I mean, Hell's Bells, where will it end?"

Now, if you need help with any of this project, you know I am still your go-to-gal. One other thing, I contacted your law firm, and they have all the instructions for my final send off, and they will contact you when it happens. I still feel real good, but, one of these days, everything could turn to, you know. Anyway, enough said!"

Dawn knew enough not to force any discussion on that subject, so they both exchanged ideas for the writer's workshop the following June.

After two-scoop turtle sundaes, it was time to leave. Audry vowed to take a nap as soon as she got home, and Dawn planned to mow the yard with Chet's tractor. With hugs and kisses, the two went their separate ways, knowing what a deep friendship was worth.

Chapter 11

Friday started off unseasonably cool for August, and Dawn was thankful for that. She had picked up the three girls at 9:00 A.M. sharp, and there was non-stop chatting on the way to ISU.
Dawn had decided to start the adventure at the Scheman building to view the first sculptor, "Gentle Doctor". All three girls were in awe of the figure, with Wren wanting to know all the facts, i.e.: when, how, and why, while Meadow worked around the sculpture, taking time to decide how to photograph it, and Lark was captured by the expression on the Doctor's face as he looked down at the dog he was holding. She could even imagine the pain the dog felt.

From there they walked northwest to the Oak and Elm Residence Halls to view the next sculpture, "Conversations". Dawn explained to the girls that the artist, Christian Petersen, took eight years to carve this piece. She continued, "It is sixty-two feet long, and was carved out of forty tons of limestone. These girls on the west end are talking to each other." Lark chimed in, "That's what girls do best!" Dawn continued, "This young man and woman are looking at a book in the center of the piece." Wren added, "I think they may have more on their minds than what is in that book!" All the girls laughed, and Dawn said, "Now, look at the girl on the east end. See how she is looking up, see the expression on her face. What do you think is crossing her mind?" All three girls were silent, contemplating, when Wren, with a smile on her face, whispered, "She is dreaming about her future, she knows she came to college to learn to live a life!" Dawn's hands flew to her heart, she was stunned. That was a phrase that Chet had written in his arrangements letter to her. She held Wren's face lightly in her hands and asked softly, "How did you come up with that, it is so beautiful?" Wren, her face blushing, answered, "I don't know, it just came to me!"

All this time, Meadow had been walking back and forth, concentrating on what image she should take. Finally, she said, "Look, you guys, see how the texture in the rock changes as the shadows cover it,

even the color changes!" Dawn suggested that Wren and Lark sit in the shade with her while Meadow finished her photography. Lark said, "O.K., but so you know, I am thinking of a chocolate malt!" Wren gave her a "look", and Dawn smiled and said, "When your sister is finished."

Twenty minutes later, Meadow announced, " I believe I have captured what I wanted. You want to see?" She shared her work on her camera screen, and they all felt that it was interesting, and told a story. Dawn commented that very few people have an eye for capturing depth and emotion, that, personally, she knew of only one person besides Meadow who could accomplish it. She then asked, " Who wants a cheeseburger, fries, and a chocolate malt?" All three girls shouted in unison, " Me!" They started their walk across campus, with their destination being the Memorial Café.

The walk took them past the President's Residence, and Dawn paused on the sidewalk that passed by the front entrance, a look of sadness coming across her face like a veil. The girls noticed that Dawn had fallen back behind them, and Wren, looking into Dawn's eyes, gently asked, " Did something happen to you here?"

Dawn, with a lump in her throat, explained, " Twenty years ago I had dinner here, and I was seated next to the most fascinating man I had ever met, a man I fell in love with, and married. He died this year, but he will always be a part of me."

Dawn then realized that all three girls had tears in their eyes, and Lark said, "We miss Mom and Dad every day, but we still love and remember them, too." As Dawn hugged them all at once, she said, "We need to be happy for the time we had with them. Now come on, I am starved!"

They arrived at the Café, and Dawn ordered four cheeseburgers, four fries, and four chocolate malts. While they were waiting for their food, Dawn noticed how the girls were absorbing their surroundings. She heard snippets of, "Cool, awesome, I feel older today," and, "I think I should come to school here someday!" Dawn felt a glow in her heart as she thought of how precious it was for these girls to have such innocence, opened to be impressed, to have unimpeded curiosity. She knew she was blessed to be here, with them, at this moment.

After they had finished lunch, Dawn revealed that the next stop would be at Parks Library. On the lower level were the sculptures of "Library Boy and Girl". When they arrived, Dawn explained, "Petersen

made these sculptures in 1944. During that time, here at ISU, boys and girls were never allowed to be in class together. The girls even had a curfew; they had to be in their dorm rooms by 7:30 each night. The only place where a boy and girl could get together to study was the library. So, girls, what do you see?"

Wren replied, "It seems that he is shy, he really wants to talk to her, but he doesn't know how to start. She is looking out of the corner of her eye at him, thinking he is cute, and wondering if he will work up enough courage to ask her out."

Lark's comments were about fashion. "Check out what they wore back in the old times. He is wearing a tie, sweater, and dress pants with cuffs. That's the kind of outfit our Dad would wear to church on Easter Sunday. And her: a blouse, sweater, skirt, and socks. Check out those shoes! Every student I have seen today was wearing an ISU T-shirt, shorts, and running shoes, or cut-off jean shorts and sandals. What a difference!"

While Dawn listened to Wren and Lark, she had noticed how quiet Meadow had been, as if she was in a deep trance, soaking it all in. When she finally talked, she said, "Look at the veins and muscles in his hands, and look at the expression in her eyes. It's like she is talking to him without speaking!"

Again, Dawn's heart skipped a beat. The last sentence that Meadow had just spoken came from a poem that Chet had written and presented to her on their fifth anniversary called *Still.*

While Meadow was photographing the sculptures, Dawn directed Wren and Lark over to the mural on the south wall. She explained, "This mural was designed by Grant Wood in 1937. It is called *Breaking the Prairie Sod.*" Wren asked, "Isn't he the man who painted the man and woman standing in front of a house, and the man is holding a pitchfork?" Dawn answered, "Yes, that painting is called *American Gothic*, and is Wood's most famous work of art.

Lark noticed that the man in the mural holding a water jug looked like Abe Lincoln, and Dawn, smiling, said, " You are right, Lark! Mr. Wood wanted to honor Mr. Lincoln because he signed the Morrill Act that helped to establish this University."

By this time Meadow had finished shooting the sculptures, and Dawn told the girls it was time to head back to the Union to look at the last sculpture, *Fountain of the Four Seasons*.

While the girls began to circle the fountain, Dawn explained that it was built in 1941, and there are

four native American women seated around the fountain at points north, south, east, and west. The first one represents the planting of seed, the next one growing the plant, the third is harvesting the bounty, and the fourth, where she is nursing her child, represents joy.

Wren commented on how peaceful and confident the women looked, Lark wanted to jump into the fountain water, and Meadow was in a quandary over how to photograph all of it.

Through all the activity around her, Dawn found herself saying a silent prayer, "Father, just a short time ago I was here for the sad experience of my husband's funeral, and now I am at the same spot with youth, energy, and a witness to inquisitive minds working full speed. Thank you!"

When Meadow had finished her photoshoot, they all went back inside the Union and Dawn bought four bottles of water, and the girls were grateful. After they all finished their water, Dawn took them to the bookstore to purchase blank journals. She explained, "Girls, these journals will serve as your text books for our classes. Your first assignment is to write about what we did today. Describe what you saw, what you felt. What did each sculpture mean to you. As we drive back to your home this afternoon, begin to organize your thoughts while they are still fresh. Then, after you've had supper and cleaned up the kitchen for Sadie, start to write in your journals. We will review them when we meet on Monday." The girls, already deep in thought, nodded their approval.

Sadie was waiting outside when they pulled into the driveway. The girls ran to their grandmother to give hugs, then inside they went. Sadie came to Dawn and said, "Thank you for caring", and Dawn quietly said , "My pleasure!"

Sadie agreed to have the girls at Dawn's home on Monday at 9:00 A.M., and as Dawn pulled out the drive, she could see the girls waving at her in the rear-view mirror, and Dawn saw herself in the mirror, a big smile on her face.

Chapter 12

Dawn prepared a light supper for herself that night, and after she had finished, she poured a cup of fresh coffee, and took it with her to Chet's office to borrow his pen. She had decided to take Audry's advice, and write to Chet. She felt it was a way to stay connected, especially during this still fragile time of mourning.

With coffee, pen, and journal in hand, she headed to the grove to sit in his chair. Somehow, she always felt closer to him each time she did this.

She began her first entry.

My dearest Chet,

Today, I put into action your wish of a writer's workshop for children. The first three attendees are Wren, age 14, Meadow, age 13, and Lark, age 12. They are sisters whose parents were killed in a car crash 2 years ago. They live with their Grandmother now, Sadie, who is a widow. You couldn't find a more wholesome soul, but at her age, 3 teenagers can wear her out.

Chet, it made me think back to my teaching days, how the students, even though they were well-mannered, could physically and mentally drain me by the end of the day.

We went to ISU to study four of Christian Petersen's sculptures. It was humbling to see how the girls viewed the art, how it touched each one of them in a different way. Their minds are so pure, so pristine, with no preconceived opinions. They just absorbed it all and let it affect them, pure and simple.

I bought them each a journal like this one, and their assignment for next Monday is to write about what we saw and felt today. I am really looking forward to reading their thoughts.

And speaking of thoughts, I know you were watching us today. Two of the girls, in conversation with me, repeated direct quotes from you, and we finished up at the fountain by the Union, where each person passed on the way to your funeral. Lover, that campus is certainly hallowed ground for you and me!

Chet, right after you passed, Audry came to comfort me. She is, and always will be, a wonderful friend. She told me how you had called her all these years twice a month to check on her. I thank you for that, and I was not surprised when she told me. I just thought, " Typical Chet!"

I still wear your shirts, your scent still lingers in them, and it gives me comfort. I miss you, I ache for you, I want and need you. and deep in my soul, I know you are watching over me.

Good night, my lover,
Dawn

She closed her journal, and her eyes, while listening to the pine boughs as they were caressed by a gentle breeze that created a symphony for lovers. She fell asleep, dreaming of butterfly kisses and blue eyes.

Chapter 13

The next morning, Dawn headed to Ames to an office supply store. She purchased an eight-foot-long banquet table and three chairs. These would be placed in Chet's office and serve as a classroom. Also on her list: twelve legal pads, eighteen pens, six three ring binders, and a hole punch. From these supplies, the girls could create their own writing portfolios.

Her next stop was the local hardware store. Three outdoor chairs and three companion tables were purchased, and would be placed in the grove, creating an outdoor classroom.

Dawn's final stop was at the grocery store, Her purchases included ham, bread, cheese, chips, cookies, ice cream, milk, malt, and chocolate syrup. At the check-out lane, the clerk raised her eyebrows at the amount of food Dawn was buying, and Dawn said, "It's for my girls!"

When she arrived back home, she noticed her message light was blinking, so after putting away the groceries, she retrieved the message. It was from Sondra Whitman who said, "Dawn, please call me. I think I have found the perfect instructor for next June's Workshop."

Dawn dialed Sondra's private number, and when Sondra answered, Dawn said, "Thank you for finding someone so quickly. But first, I want to tell you what I started this week."

She went on to explain about the three girls, the program, and what she envisioned the future to be. Sondra commented, "It sounds like this is as good for you as it is for them. I feel there is a new children's book in the making!" Dawn laughed and said, "Who did you find for the instructor position?" Sondra began to explain, "His name is Christopher Cody. He was born on September 20,1988. His mother is Katherine Cody, one of the original employees of a software company called Microsoft, and yes she had a block of the original stock. His bio never mentions a father. Chris attended Northwest Academy in Portland, Oregon, where his high school thesis was *Crisis of the American Story Teller.* He went on to Portland State, and graduated in 2008, and yes, he did it in three years, with honors. He had some short stories published while attending college, and in 2010, he was awarded the *National New Emerging Author* award.

Along with short stories and a novel, he is also a published poet, I have seen his work, and was surprised at the depth of emotion he writes with, like he has an old soul." Dawn interjected, "Sondra, that sounds like someone we both knew." There was a moment of silence, then Sondra, in a choked-up voice said, "I know. I miss coming into the office to read Chet's newest chapters. I could always count on going through a box of tissues, and having a big smile on my face. He was one-of-a-kind." And Dawn whispered, "Amen."

Sondra continued, "I am trying to add Chris to our stable of authors, but no luck so far. Why don't you think about this and call me in a week. I will keep the lines of communication open with Chris. Good luck with your project with the girls! Bye for now."

Dawn hung up the phone and thought that this young author might be the perfect choice as the instructor. She then made a short entry into her journal.

Darling,

I just got off the phone with Sondra. She has found a candidate for the position of guest instructor for the Chester T. Carrington Writer's Workshop. His bio shows that he is very smart and productive, and I am thinking he could put a fresh slant on writing for the other authors.

He is from Portland, Oregon. I remember one time we were having a conversation, and you brought up the fact that it is always wet , cold, and gloomy in Portland in December.

Anyway, the three girls will be here in the morning, so I need to get a good night's rest.

Dreaming of you!

Chapter 14

Sadie was right on time delivering the girls on Monday. Dawn met them in the driveway and received a hug from each one. They told their Grandmother goodbye, and Dawn said, "How about a tour of my place. Bring your journals, and we will start in the office.

As soon as the girls went through the door, the questions began from Wren, "What are all those binders for?" Dawn replied, "Chet would take notes of all the research he would conduct in preparation of writing a novel. The finished manuscripts of his five, *New York Times* best selling books are there. There are some that contain only poetry, and there is also one that contains a finished novel that he never allowed to be published. I remember him saying, "I have spent the majority of my life writing for others. This one is by me, for me."

Meadow asked, "So, what's it about?" Dawn replied, "I have no idea. He never asked me to read it, and I loved and respected him enough not to inquire."

What Dawn did not reveal is that Chet had left instructions in his will that stated if Dawn ever fell into financial hardship in the future, she had the legal right to have the novel published.

Sondra Whitman was the only other person who knew the novel existed, and Dawn knew she could count on her discretion.

Lark chimed in, "So, is this like our classroom? Is this where we will become famous authors? Are these pads and pens for us to use?" Dawn, with a laugh, answered, "Yes, that is up to you, and yes. Now come on, I want to show all of you the other classroom. Just leave your journals on the table."

They all headed down to the pine grove, and upon arriving, each girl sat in a new chair, and Dawn sat in her Adirondack, leaving Chet's empty. Wren quietly said, "That was his chair, wasn't it? I wonder how many ideas came to him while he sat there. Sadie tells us you don't always have to be in church to talk to God, you can be in other places, too! I think this was one of those places for Chet." Dawn thought,

From the mouths of babes comes truth. She answered Wren, "Yes, we spent countless hours here, many of them without speaking, just listening to the sounds the boughs make when the wind blows through. It is also a world-class place to take a nap, so I've been told!" All the girls grinned, and Dawn continued, "Let's go back and I will show you the inside of the house, and there are some chocolate chip cookies that need to be eaten. Any volunteers?"

With a "Yes!" in unison, the girls walked, hand in hand towards the house, with Dawn just steps behind, grinning.

After their snack, Dawn took the girls back to the classroom in the office. She began, "Open your journals, and let's discuss what you have written." The girls talked about the different sculptures, how each one gave them a different feeling or meaning. Lark was really enthralled with "Gentle Doctor". She said, "I don't know who is in more pain, the dog or the doctor. You can tell the dog is feeling bad, but the look on the doctor's face, even the way he is holding the dog, says he feels sorry for it, that he just wants to make it feel better." Dawn told Lark that those were great observations, then Meadow said, "My turn." She went on to say her favorites were "Library Boy and Girl", that the figures looked almost alive, and, "If you looked real close, it was like you could see a pulse in their veins. Plus, their facial expressions were like they were talking without saying a word." She asked Dawn, "Is that even possible?"

Dawn paused then answered, "Yes, it is. Textbooks would call it non-verbal communication. I call it a part of loving someone." After hearing that, Lark rolled her eyes, saying, "Whatever!"

Wren knew it was her turn, and she began by talking about the girl who sat at the end of the wall in "Conversations".

She began, "First of all, the title is 'Conversations', and the kids on one end are probably talking about classes, or an upcoming test, the couple leaning over a book in the middle are thinking about each other, but the girl on the end, by herself, is a mystery. There is no one for her to talk to, she is just looking up into the sky." Dawn asked Wren, "Can you have a conversation with someone, even if you can't see them? If you are thinking about your future, is that a conversation with yourself? What if she is talking to God, is that a conversation?" Wren replied, "Too many questions, not enough answers. I need to ponder this some more."

Dawn took the girls back to the house for lunch. They made ham and cheese sandwiches, and Dawn made chocolate malts.

After they finished, Dawn gave them an assignment for the afternoon. Each one of them needed to pick a character from the sculptures, and make them come alive. She suggested that they should go to the grove and work there. Lark said, "Did someone say that was a good place to nap?" Dawn laughed, as she said, "O.K., head on down there. I have some business calls to make, and I will join you shortly." As she watched them navigate to the grove, she could tell their imaginations were in high gear.

Dawn's first phone call was to Sondra, who had left a message when class was in session. When she answered, she said, "Dawn, I have great news. Christopher Cody was just awarded the top prize from the Poetry Society of America for his poem titled *Missed.* I am going to e-mail you a copy, it gave me goose-bumps when I read it. I called to congratulate him, and I think he is waiting for your invitation to instruct next year. He is a devoted fan of Chet's body of work, he said his mother always had those books in their home, and he would consider it an honor to be in his shadow. I will include his phone number in the e-mail. How are the girls?"

Dawn told her about the project they were working on right now, and would keep her informed. She thanked Sondra for the information, and would look forward to receiving the e-mail, then said goodbye.

After paying a few bills and picking up the kitchen, Dawn made her way to the grove. When they caught sight of her, they all began talking at once. Dawn laughed and said, " O.K., what gives?"

Wren gave both Meadow and Lark a "look", than started. "We all came up with an idea for a short story. How about this? Each year, on the Fourth of July, when the bells on the Campanile strike midnight, the figures on the sculptures come alive, and make their way across Campus. The two from the library reach out and hold hands, and when they get outside, they walk slowly towards the sound of the ringing bells.

The gentle doctor walks out of his building holding the dog. After he crosses the street, he puts a leash on the dog and sets it down on the grass, and they head towards Central Campus. When they arrive at the Campanile, he frees the dog, who then runs circles around him, jumping and barking, enjoying his freedom."

Meadow jumped in, "My turn. The three girls on the west end of 'Conversations' come to life, they all stretch, like they are reaching for the stars, and they all head to State Gym to play a game of basketball."

Lark adds, "The couple in the middle of that sculpture pick up the book that they were supposedly reading, hold hands, and walk to the library. They run into Library Boy and Girl who are walking in the opposite direction, and say to them, "We are so bored with this book, we need to check out another one."

Dawn was very impressed with the girls' ideas, but asked, "What about the girl on the east end of 'Conversations'?" Wren replied, "The three basketball girls asked her to join them, but she declined, saying she was going to just stretch her limbs and stay put, she was still waiting for an answer.

When the library kids made it to the Campanile, the bells were still ringing, so they kiss and become true Iowa Staters." Lark made a face and said, with protest, "How mushy can you get!"

Meadow took Dawn's hand, then asked, "Were you and Chet Staters?" and Dawn replied, "Yes, many times over, we found practice makes perfect." To which Lark piped up, "Too much information!"

Dawn asked all of them, "Why did you pick the fourth of July?" All three girls looked at her, and, in unison, said, "Independence Day!", and Dawn smacked her forehead and said "Duh!"

They all laughed and hugged, and Dawn reminded them, "Come on, it's time for Sadie to pick you up. Since you all start school next week, the next time I will see you is a week from Saturday." Sadie pulled in the drive, and while the girls climbed into the car, Dawn reached through the driver's window, patted Sadie's hand, and whispered, "Thank you."

The girls all waved goodbye as the car went out the driveway, and Dawn headed into the house to write in her journal.

Chapter 15

Honey,

The girls just left, and, again, it was just a pure pleasure being with them. They came up with an idea of writing a short story that revolves around the Petersen sculptures we saw the other day, I envy their ability to use imagination as a tool, totally uninhibited by life experience, not tainted in any way.

My love, we never spent a lot of time talking about having children. I just assumed that if it were meant to be, it would happen. I do wish, for your sake, that either Michelle or I could have made an heir with you, to pass along all the wonderful traits that made you who you are, but we can't wish away our lives.

Maybe the master plan is in play now. I am here to help with these three incredible girls, to help guide them, to support their efforts, and help give meaning to their lives.

I just hope that I don't make any mistakes; it has been a hell of a long time since I was addressed as " Teacher."

Thinking of you always,
Dawn

Chapter 16

Later that day, Dawn finally turned on her computer and found the e-mail from Sondra that included the poem by Christopher Cody. She printed a copy and laid it on the kitchen table. She had decided to take a walk up the road, stretching her legs and clearing her mind. She believed in the saying , "You only get the first impression once", and she wanted to be razor sharp when she read the poem for the first time. Her decision to accept, or reject, Christopher Cody as the inaugural speaker for the workshop hinged on the emotions that his poem brought out in her.

Dawn knew it wasn't quite fair, she had been married to the master of emotions for twenty years, but it would be interesting to see how Chris measured up. She poured a glass of merlot, sat at the table, and began to read.

Missed

My Father and I never met
Half of who I am
Came from a mystery man
He never felt the scar on my knee
From my fall from a tree
I never felt that reassurance a son gets from a pat
On the head
From a Dad
Who missed
Roughhousing, wrestling, touch football, having a catch
Those father and son talks that came on long walks
Skipping flat stones across mirror surfaced lakes
The very first time I took a girl on a date
All were missed

Fathers are suppose to blaze a trail for a son to follow
Leaving markers and advice along the way
Where do I find the start?
If it was left, unmarked
Did I cross his path?
Did I not recognize his sign?
Have we brushed against each other on a crowed street?
Time after time
Or has that been missed

Is his nose my nose?
Are his eyes my eyes?
Will I see what he has seen?
Are the troubles I'll face ahead ones he has already met
Is my voice his voice?
Have I heard what he has said?
Do I say what he would say?
Did he ever cry for me?
As I cried for him
Or has that been missed

My hands are young while his are old
Are they still limber?
Or calloused and cold
My posture is upright
Is his bent forward from the wear and weight of life?
Or is he lying down in peace

If I am blessed with a son
One-fourth of him will be from you
Dad
Will you see?
Will you know?
From heaven
Or will that
Be missed
By
You

Christopher Cody 2012

Dawn was rendered speechless, tears streamed down her cheeks. She took another drink of wine, and read the poem again. By the end, her thoughts were, "How could a person this young write with the depth and feeling of a seasoned and life-experienced person, a person with an old soul? To not only express pain and loss, but also show an inner strength to carry on, while looking back."

She decided, at that moment, that Christopher was the perfect choice to be the instructor to honor Chet's memory. Destiny had surely brought them together in the grand plan.

Dawn finished her wine, got up from the table to pour a cup of coffee, and then called Sondra. When she answered, Dawn began, "I read the poem, I cried, and read it again. It went to my inner core, touching all of my emotions. My next call will be to Chris, issuing the invitation to teach at the workshop. With his ability to write poetry, in addition to his works of fiction, a new standard will be set for literature. Sondra, thank you for leading me to him!"

Sondra responded, "I am glad I could assist you, please let me know if he accepts." They said their goodbyes, then Dawn placed the call that would forever change her life.

To Dawn's surprise, Chris picked up the phone on the second ring, and in a low, soft voice, said, "This is Chris, how may I help you?"

Dawn replied, "Chris, this is Dawn Carrington. I was referred to you by Sondra Whitman. I just finished reading your poem, *MISSED,* and I must say, it was a deeply moving experience. I would like to offer you the guest lecturer position at the Chester Carrington Memorial Workshop to be held next June at Iowa State University."

After a few moments of silence, Chris replied, "Thank you for the kind words about my poem. I would consider it an honor to accept your offer. I have been a fan of your husband's work all of my young life. My mother always has at least one of his books on a coffee table, or in the library. Personally, my attempts at poetry pale to the classic that Chet penned, *Sweep the Floor Clean.* Please send me the schedule, and if possible, I would like to come out a few days earlier to walk the ground where Chet walked. Again, Dawn, thank you for this opportunity. I know my mother will be excited."

Dawn assured him that she would make all the arrangements, and would forward all the information he would need. After she hung up, she called Sondra and left a message, simply saying, "It's done. He accepted."

Dawn refilled her coffee cup, put on one of his flannel shirts, picked up her journal and a pen, and made her way to the grove. Sitting in his chair, she wrote:

My dearest Lover,

We found him. Sondra started the process, and I finished it. He is Christopher Cody from Portland, Oregon. At age 24, he thinks and writes like you did in your 50's. I just read a poem that won him a national award, and I invited him to be the instructor at the workshop. This will raise the bar in American literature, and I am so proud that your name will be associated with it.

Missing you!
Dawn

Chapter 17

The next days flew by until it was Saturday, and Sadie had dropped off the girls at Dawn's house. After all the hugs, they went to the classroom. Dawn asked them to share what they had written in their journals since she last saw them, and they each read aloud their entries. A majority of it was comprised of things that had happened at school, who moved out, who moved in, and how were this year's teachers. When Dawn inquired if there were any cute boys, the girls all said no.

Then Dawn said, "Meadow, I am so glad you brought your camera. Today we are going to Story City to ride the Carousel. I'll fill you in on it's history, on the drive there. After that, we will eat lunch, then stop at the Norseman Art Gallery to see the newest exhibit. Let's load up and head out!"

As Dawn drove, she explained the Carousel history, "It was made in Tonawanda, New York, by the Herschell-Spillman company in 1913. All of the animals are hand-carved, and they consist of 20 horses, 2 chickens, 2 pigs, 2 dogs, and 2 chariots. A calliope plays music while the Carousel spins around."

By the time they arrived, the girls were primed to have a good time. Wren started out on a horse, Meadow, a chariot, and Lark, on the chicken. Around and around they would go, switching mounts constantly, as their laughter filled the air. Dawn's smile widened as she thought, "I had forgotten how contagious a child's laughter is. Pure enjoyment, no foreseeable troubles!"

After two hours, the girls were ready for lunch. Dawn decided to stay away from the fast food places out by I-35, and went into town to the Royal Café. It was turkey, mashed potatoes, gravy, and green beans all around. While they waited for their order, Wren asked Dawn, "Would it be O.K. if we came up with a short story about the Carousel, like we did with the sculptors?" Dawn thought, "YES!" She replied, "That sounds like a great subject. What are your thoughts?" The imagination flow was turned on, and all through lunch, between bites, ideas overflowed.

Lark suggested that at night, all the animals on the Carousel change position to confuse the ride operator when he saw them in the morning.

Meadow wanted all the animals to escape at night, and they would go to a magic pasture, where the grass was head high, concealing them. They could eat their fill and sleep in the fresh night's air.

Wren wanted to combine the Carousel with the sculptures from ISU. She said, "What if, on the night of July 4th, the sculpture people meet at the Campanile, borrow a Cy-Ride bus, and come here for their own private party. They would ride the Carousel until the first ray of light was seen from the east, and they would rush back to campus. After sunrise, the students would comment that the figures seemed to have larger smiles than last week. And they would have no idea why!"

Dawn, shaking her head in amazement said, "Excellent start! Work out the details, make notes in your journals, and write your story. The possibilities are endless!"

When Dawn went to pay the bill, her waitress said, "If you don't mind me saying so, your daughters are about the best behaved kids I have ever seen, and so happy, too!" Dawn smiled and replied, "I am blessed. Thank you."

Their next stop was the Norseman Art Gallery. When they entered, Chuck, Karen, and Lou greeted them. They gave the girls hugs all around, and each one of them paired off with one of the girls, so they could explain the exhibit , which was put on by the 4-H Camera Corps. The core subject was "American Life", and the contestants took photos all year long to capture an image that would fit the theme. The top forty photos were hanging in the gallery, and any person who came to the gallery could vote for "Best of Show".

While the girls circled the gallery, trying to pick their favorite image, Dawn found a chair in the corner, sat down, and closed her eyes. She remembered the night Chet brought her here, how he had reserved the gallery that night just for them. On the walls were paintings of angels, and he said, "Lover, tonight we are surrounded by angels of all shapes and sizes. The most beautiful one in the room is you. Saving me was an act of mercy on your part, and I will be eternally grateful to you for showing me how to love again. Would you grant me the honor of being your wedded husband? "As Dawn wiped away the tears that were flowing down her cheeks, she remembered her response, "Yes, and what took you so long?"

The girls noticed her wiping her eyes, and asked what was wrong. Dawn replied, "I was just remembering, and these are tears of joy! Now, have all of you voted for the best of show? We need to get home so Sadie can pick you up."

They all cast their ballots, thanked the volunteers, and piled into Dawn's car. They made it back home just before Sadie pulled into the driveway. They said their goodbyes, and Dawn told them she would see them in two weeks, and she would be looking forward to reading their new stories.

For Dawn, it had been a tiring, yet fulfilling day. The last thing to do before she went to bed was to write another entry in her journal to Chet.

To my best friend,

Today was another fun-filled day with the girls. Our first stop was at the Carousel. They rode every animal, all 28 of them, laughing the whole time.

Chet, I remember after we became lovers, you paid to have a private session on that ride for just the two of us. God, what wonderful memories we made together!

After lunch, I took the girls to the Gallery, and while they toured the exhibit, I had the luxury of my emotions being washed by the memory of the night you proposed to me there. I can still hear the music; the string duet played; still catch the scent of the perfect, single red rose in a crystal vase on the one table in the room, all of it wrapped in the love you had for me.

I give thanks each and every night for the time we had, together.

With never ending love,
Dawn

Chapter 18

Earlier in the week Dawn had called Harry and Alice and asked them if they would open up the cabin for the following week. Harry assured her it would be ready by next Monday, and Dawn thanked him.

She planned to pick up the house on Sunday, after church, and spend the afternoon packing clothes for the trip. She set her suitcase on the kitchen table, put her journal and his pen on top, and went to sleep.

It was a beautiful fall day, with the birch trees just starting to change color, when she arrived at the cabin. After unpacking, she made a pot of coffee and uncovered the piano. She said, aloud, "Hello old friend, let's see if I can remember all the things Mother had taught me."

She played till after dark and went to bed with a warm, satisfied feeling, whispering to her Mom, "I can still play."

She spent the next ten days on Black Duck, playing piano, taking *Author* out to the falls, sitting outside, listening to the leaves rustle as the wind gently stirred, and each night, just before sunset, she would stroll up the knoll to visit the graves of Chet and Michelle. She would lean down, and brush the leaves off the grave stones, and thank Michelle for teaching "our man" how to love. She would tell Chet that she was getting along rather well, the pain of loss was not as intense, and she felt that he had been watching over her all this time. She would then whisper, "God bless both of you, as he has blessed me."

By the time Dawn's ten days were up, she was looking forward to seeing the girls, and to hear what was new in their lives. She thanked Harry and Alice, and set out for home.

Chapter 19

On the Sunday that Dawn packed for her trip, Christopher Cody was at his mother's penthouse in Portland, Oregon. After he had graduated from Portland State, Katherine said, " Chris, I would like to start a new family tradition. Would you consent to being at the penthouse the third Sunday of each month for dinner? I would give the staff the day off, and that would give me a chance to cook for you."

Chris replied, " Mother, you make it sound like one of your corporate mergers. I would be glad to see you and have dinner. I will arrive at 11:00 A.M. on Sunday."

Katherine had made a pot roast, and Chris was welcomed by the smells of comfort food. While they were eating, Chris announced, " Mother, I have some exciting news. I have been invited to be the guest instructor at the Chester Carrington Memorial Writer's Workshop at Iowa State University next June. The invitation came personally from Dawn Carrington, Chet's widow. She had read my poem, *Missed,* and decided that I would lead the workshop in a new direction. Mother, do we still have some of Carrington's books here?" Katherine replied, " I believe there are a few in the library. I actually met him in person. Let's see, I think it was in December of 1987, at a book signing held at Powell's Book Store downtown. Rumor was that he had been in seclusion for two years, but his publisher needed him back on the book signing tour. I remember he put on a good front for the public, but he seemed old and lonely. Anyway, congratulations on your invitation, you continue to make me proud! More gravy?"

They continued to visit over dinner, and Katherine filled Chris in on the details of a winery at the foot of Mt. Hood that she had just invested in as a silent partner. She explained that it would make a nice addition to Chris's trust fund.

Chapter 20

It was a Saturday classroom day, and as soon as Sadie stopped the car, the three girls ran to Dawn for a group hug. Sadie called out, "They have been marking off the days on the calendar, saying " Two more, then, one more" Thank you, Dawn, and I will be back for them at 4:00 P.M.

Dawn informed the girls that they were going to Reiman Gardens at ISU and she couldn't wait for the girls to experience the butterfly wing. She asked them to leave their journals in the office. They would work on them in the afternoon.

When they arrived, their first stop was the Christina Reiman Butterfly Wing. They had to pass through a double door airlock entry, so the butterflies wouldn't escape.

Once inside, the girl's eyes got as big as saucers! Meadow was in her zone, camera in hand, trying to decide what to photograph first. Wren was as interested in the foliage as she was in the butterflies.

Lark was sitting on a bench with Dawn, absolutely mesmerized by the rainbow of colors that the butterflies displayed.

A Monarch drifted down gently, landing on the back of her neck, and she exclaimed, "Dawn, look at my neck, it feels like he is kissing me when he flutters his wings!"

Dawn's memory instantly flashed back to that fateful day on Black Duck, when a butterfly landed on the nape of her neck, and she knew. She replied to Lark, "He is showing you how much he loves you." And Lark quipped, "Hey you, we just met!"

After the two hour adventure, Dawn told the girls it was time to go to Hickory Park for lunch, followed by Turtle Sundaes, and there were no objections.

On the drive home, after lunch, Meadow asked if they could use some of the images she had taken that morning in their short story, and Wren thought there might be some more characters to add, after what they had seen at the Garden.

Dawn commented, "I just love it when you girls use your imagination. Please promise me that you will never loose that quality." And they replied, in unison, "Why would we?"

The rest of the afternoon was spent down in the grove, tossing back and forth ideas about potential stories, which seemed to be in a constant stream of change.

Sadie announced her presence with the honk of her car horn, and the girls left, reminding Dawn they would be back in two weeks.

After they departed, Dawn noticed how quiet it was. She went inside the house, opened a bottle of merlot that Christopher Cody had sent her from a winery in Portland, filled her glass, and began another journal entry.

Chet, you rascal!

I took the girls to Reiman Gardens today, and while we were in the butterfly wing, a Monarch landed on Lark's neck, and she described the feeling as if its wings were kissing her. In my heart, I knew it was you checking in, making sure everything was O.K. Thank you, my love, for that.

We stopped and ate lunch at Hickory Park, and yes, you should feel proud about my restraint, just one Sundae! Things are going smoothly here, and I give thanks each night for God's guidance, and your love.

Good night, lover,
Dawn

Chapter 21

The weeks rolled by for Dawn, and it seemed to her that she had never been this busy. There was all the lawn work that Chet always did, plus the regular house cleaning. Each week she would have a hour long conversation with Audry on the phone, and every two weeks, they would meet for lunch.

Their last lunch was at the Happy Chef in Story City. Of course, Audry arrived first, and even though Dawn was five minutes early, Audry said, "Maybe you should save some money so you can buy a watch that tells the right damn time!" Dawn just grinned, this was just Audry being herself. Halfway through lunch, Audry commented, "Old age doesn't sneak up on me any more, it's here, right now. I feel like my father's old 1949 International truck, no springs in the rear, and super low first gear. It takes me forever to get from point A to point B. I guess it beats taking an eternal dirt nap. Enough said about that."

She was always interested in what Dawn had to say about the girls, how her face lit up as she told their stories, and Audry knew, without a doubt, that they were Dawn's saving grace.

Dawn said the girls had continued to come by every other Saturday, and she had taken them to movies, a piano concert at C.Y. Stephens Auditorium, and a play at the Des Moines Playhouse.

And the short story they had started together had become anything but short. Their imaginations had free rein, and the journals were now filled with ninety pages of ideas. Dawn was hesitant to have them start to organize their story. She didn't want to squash the creative process. Audry had agreed, commenting, " Give them their heads, let them run with it. Remember, destiny will guide them."

Dawn also kept Audry up-to-date on the writers workshop. All twenty of the writers who were invited had accepted. Chris had asked that anyone who felt inclined could submit a poem on any subject. Chris would critique them, and then give positive comments at the workshop.

Dawn continued to explain to Audry that all the arrangements for food and housing for the authors were complete, plus airline tickets and car rentals. A suite had been booked for Chris for ten days, so he could spend time touring the campus, and learn more about Chet. Audry, asked, "If it is not much trouble, I would like to take you and Chris out to dinner when he is here, I'd like to pick his brain, see what makes him tick." Dawn agreed. She then suggested, "We better head for home, this lunch turned into a three hour gab fest." In the parking lot, Audry took Dawn's hands in hers, looked her straight in the eyes, and whispered, in a choked-up voice, "You have been everything to me since we met, all those years ago. Thank you for being the daughter I never had." And Dawn replied, holding back her tears, "It has always been a pleasure, and like you say, it was destined to happen."

Chapter 22

Sadie had demanded that Dawn have Thanksgiving dinner with her and the girls, and Dawn was elated by the invitation.

As soon as she stepped through the front door, her senses were welcomed by the aroma of turkey, stuffing, green bean casserole, gravy, homemade noodles, and three kinds of pie: pumpkin, apple, and cherry. Those three were served with home churned ice cream.

As usual, conversations at the dinner table with the girls were far reaching, from school to boys, sports, and their story ideas.

When dinner was over, Sadie asked the girls to clean up. Then she asked Dawn to join her in the parlor. After she slid the two large oak doors together, Sadie said, "I have some things I need to say to you, just listen, and then you can consider your options.

You have been a blessing to both me, and the girls. They seem more content, more grounded, and are even more responsible than they were when they first moved here. I am not getting any younger, so I paid your friend, Jenny Black, over at the Human Service Department in the Court House, a visit. I explained my idea to her, and both of us went to the bank and met with a Trust officer.

So Dawn, here's the deal. I have placed all my assets in a trust account. I get the income from it as long as I live. Upon my death, the income will go to the three girls in equal shares. I want you to become their legal guardian at the time, and if you wish, and the girls agree, you may adopt them. Jenny has all the legal paperwork done, sitting in a file.

When you decide, I will go in and sign the forms. All I ask is that you take some time to consider this offer. You are the only person I would entrust their future to. Now, let's go eat some pie."

Dawn was stunned. Sadie had just presented her with a most precious gift, and her heart swelled, knowing Sadie would trust her to that extent. She would take time to seriously consider the opportunity, since it had the potential to be a life-changing event for her, personally.

Dawn joined the girls and Sadie for pie, and told them she would be spending Christmas at Black Duck, and they would resume their classes with her after the first of the year. Kisses and hugs followed dessert, and Dawn headed home, her mind already reviewing what the prospects would be if she accepted Sadie's offer.

Upon arriving at home, Dawn made coffee, took Chet's heavy leather coat out of the closet, bundled up, and headed to the grove.

She sat in his chair and began speaking, "Honey, I was presented a wonderful opportunity today. If anything happens to Sadie, she wants me to take her granddaughters and raise them. I know it is a daunting responsibility, so I am looking for some guidance on this. Please help me if you can. Thanks, lover."

Dawn finished her coffee, turned up the collar on his coat, and slowly headed back to the house. Before she went to sleep, she read one of Chet's poems again, *Sweep the Floor Clean,* and felt comfort.

Chapter 23

It was Christmas morning on Black Duck Lake, and Dawn woke up to a chill inside the cabin. She had arrived late the night before, and had neglected to turn up the thermostat. By the time her coffee was made, the furnace had raised the temperature to a toasty seventy-five degrees.

She had decided to come here for one purpose. It was the first wedding anniversary without Chet. Twenty-two years ago, on this day, Pastor Hutton had officiated at the marriage ceremony, right here in the cabin. It was time for her to reflect, so she pulled out her journal, along with his pen, and began to write:

Darling,

I am here in our cabin, warm and toasty, on the anniversary of our wedding. I am not going to cry, or wring my hands, or feel sorry for myself. Today, I am going to celebrate our life together, and the deep passionate love we shared.

Honey, your presence surrounds me. I am wearing one of your flannel shirts with a frayed left cuff, your body scent woven into the fabric.

I lift my eyes to the wall in the great room and immerse myself in the portrait you commissioned from a photoshoot taken the night you proposed. God, we looked so young back then. Yet, when I study our faces in that portrait, the love that comes through is a love that never faltered, it only grew deeper, richer, more fulfilling then I could ever imagined.

Chet, we were so fortunate, not one cross or vindictive word was uttered by either one of us against the other. For years, people would comment to me that we seemed to get along so well. My answer was always the same. We had mutual respect for each other, and we never kept score, then I would smile at them, and they always looked bewildered.

Lover, I know that if we had never met, I would not be the person that I am today. We took all the good from each other and intertwined it into our souls. We had the perfect recipe, we fulfilled each other without ever feeling used.

And God, the romance! We definitely cornered the market on that. All those little things we did for each other. Those touches from you that would ignite a glow deep inside me, how you knew the exact spots on my body that would drive me insane!

Candlelight suppers, even if the fare was beans and franks, when you would look across the table into my eyes, and I knew that I was the only thing on your mind, and in your heart.

My dearest, my admiration for your writings never wavered, it just grew deeper as we matured together. The way you could write about feelings and emotions were a skill that can't be learned, it is a talent given to only a few. And with that talent, you strived to touch other people's lives. I can only imagine that when you entered Heaven, God said, "You served me well."

So today, I am going to let my mind just wander through the field of memories that we grew, filling all my senses, savoring it all.

I will play my Mom's piano, and think of her.

I will sing "Saving Grace", the one you asked me to write for you, with love.

I will walk up to the knoll to visit you and Michelle, and thank her for loving you, and letting you love me.

I will sleep tonight, warm and cozy, wrapped in the comfort of our life, our love.

Yours forever,
Dawn

Chapter 24

Dawn enjoyed the holiday in quiet solitude at the lake, but for some unknown reason, she knew she should be back at home before January 1st. Perhaps it was an inner feeling of starting the New Year with a clean slate, no lingering problems or baggage.

She was so looking forward to seeing the girls, having lunch with Audry, and fine tuning the upcoming writers workshop.

On the drive back home, there was one other thought that came to her. The grief from loosing Chet had been as if a surgeon had operated on her heart and soul. The layers of stitches were left behind, and the healing had taken a long time. The pain went from intolerable to manageable, and now, just occasional discomfort. There would always be an emotional scar, a reminder of her strength and fortitude. She was content knowing that she had survived the ordeal, and had become even stronger.

The drive home proved to be relaxing. There was no snow or ice on the roads, and she made good time.

After settling in at the house, with a fresh cup of coffee, Dawn played the messages in her voicemail. The girls had called and sang *Noel* in beautiful, three part harmony, Sadie had left a Merry Christmas greeting, and Audry said, "Well, another Christmas Day is behind us, and I have never seen so many old people, including myself, drain a 5 gallon bowl of eggnog. How about lunch the first Friday after New Years. I still need to continue my search for the best pork tenderloin sandwich in Iowa. Give me a call." The Gallery crew had left their good wishes, and Sondra had said she wanted to fly out in the spring to visit.

The final message was from Robert Cheetum, one of the attorneys that represented Chet's estate. He asked to meet with Dawn on the morning of January 2nd. He would drive up from Ames to meet, and would 9:00 A.M. work for her.

Before Dawn retired for the night, she wrote herself a note to return Cheetum's call in the morning. With positive hopes for the New Year, Dawn slept with a smile on her face.

Chapter 25

The following morning, Dawn did call the law office. Their voicemail said the office was closed for the holidays, and they would be open on January 2nd. She left a message that she would meet Mr. Cheetum on the morning of the 2nd, as per his request.

She then began a through tour of her home, making a list of possible changes she might make to the decorating scheme.

When they were first married, Chet had given her an option to change anything she wanted in the house. She thanked him for his offer, but said it was fine for now. Well, Dawn thought, "For now turned into 22 years."

Her list included:

- *New bathroom fixtures*
- *Tile bathroom floor*
- *Change paint colors in living and dining room-Teal & Tan?*
- *New curtains all around-energy efficient*
- *Repaint front door-consider fire engine red!!!*

One thing she would never change was his office. Dawn knew it had to remain just as he left it. That thought reminded her to return his pen to the top of his desk, on the legal pad.

January 1st came, cold but clear. Dawn spent time browsing through all the seed catalogs that had come in the mail the past two months. She added to her list:

- *Increase size of garden*
- *Check out Heirloom Tomato seeds*

Late in the afternoon, she enjoyed some new cheese varieties Sondra had sent, along with another bottle of wine that Chris had shipped from Oregon.

Before retiring to bed for the night, Dawn returned Audry's call. It went to voicemail, and Dawn said, "I have heard that a great tenderloin can be found at Niland's Café in Colo, on the old Lincoln Highway. Lets meet there on Friday at noon. Bye for now."

One more glass of Chris's wine, and Dawn was ready for a good night's sleep.

Chapter 26

The following morning brought a chill inside the house. Dawn looked outside at the thermometer, which read 0 degrees, and she saw the trees were bending from a strong wind. A quick check of the TV weather mentioned a wind chill of minus 20.

Her next instinct was to crawl back under the covers, but she remembered her 9:00 appointment, so she took a steamy hot shower, dressed, and waited.

Robert Cheetum arrived exactly at 9:00, and Dawn welcomed him in. She noticed he carried in two medium sized boxes, along with his briefcase, from which, after sitting at the kitchen table, he withdrew an envelope.

After a polite exchange of pleasantries and cups of coffee, Robert began, "Dawn, I am here today to serve my client, Audry Chance. I am fulfilling her last request to deliver her final instructions to you. I want to express my sympathy to you for your loss." Dawn seemed to be in a fog, she did not understand what he had just said. She thought, "I must have had too much wine last night." With panic taking over her voice, she said, "This must be a mistake. Audry is fine, she left me a voicemail on Christmas day, and I returned her call just last night, leaving her a message. We are having lunch on Friday!"

Robert Cheetum reached across the table to hold Dawn's hand. In a quiet voice, he said, "Audry passed away the day after Christmas. When she didn't arrive for breakfast that morning, one of the staff members at her retirement home went to her suite with a pass key, and found Audry in her bed, as if she had gone to sleep and never woke up. The medical examiner who was called said it looked like she had a heart attack, and she did not suffer at all."

Dawn's head was spinning with misbelief. She asked, "Why wasn't I informed when it happened?" Cheetum replied, "Audry left very strict instructions. I was the contact person, and I was to call the funeral home. She had arranged to be cremated, and no one was to be notified of her death until that was done."

"Dawn, in one of these boxes is a sealed urn. It contains her remains. I have no idea what is in the smaller box, my instructions were to deliver both at the same time, along with this sealed letter from Audry.

I will leave now, so you can open them in private. If you have any questions later, please call me, at any time. Again, I am so sorry for your loss. I will let myself out."

And with that, Dawn was left, alone, at her kitchen table, two boxes and a letter to be opened, and a deep feeling that the wound that had finally healed had just been ripped open, allowing fresh, excruciating pain, to flow in.

Chapter 27

It was as if shock had invaded Dawn's body. In front of her sat a box that contained the ashes of her oldest and dearest friend. Audry had been through it all with Dawn, her rock to lean on during her early teaching career, the person who would not sugar coat the truth, the one person who had the faith that Dawn would find true love. And after all of that, she was left with two boxes and an envelope to open. With tears streaming down her face, she opened the letter and recognized Audry's perfect penmanship. It began:

Dawn,

If you are reading this, then I must no longer be among the living. You are the only person I would trust to clean up after my demise. Thank you for that.

I left instructions with the attorney that no one should be notified about my death until I was cremated. I always had an inversion to people viewing someone laid out in a casket in clothes they rarely wore while they were living. So, now you know why.

Financially, all final expenses have been paid. I took care of that one year ago. The balance of all my money will transfer into an endowment fund managed by the attorney. Each year, a $5,000 scholarship will be awarded to the Homecoming Queen at Westside High. I figure that it will take fifty years to exhaust the fund, and by that time, there won't be one damn soul in that town who will remember who I was.

If, by chance, the school closes, or is consolidated, the balance of the fund will go to the Parks Library at ISU to purchase first editions of modern day poets. It will be called the Audry Chance Special Collection. That is one hell of a mouthful! Maybe some student will read one poem, and have their life take a different direction. I can only hope!

Honey, in the smaller box is something very precious to me, and I wanted you to have it. Go ahead and open it now, I can wait.

Dawn dried her eyes and opened the box. Inside was a letter-sized cedar box that looked familiar to her. After opening it, she remembered. Inside was a single pearl mounted on a gold band. This was Audry's engagement ring from Roger Hemstead, and the letter, the one that seemed to have been folded a thousand times, the one where he explained, in 1952, that the engagement was off. Dawn read it, and the result was like rubbing salt into an open wound. She put the letter and ring back in the box, and continued with Audry's letter:

All right, now that you have seen them, here is what I want you to do. The ring is for you to wear, if you choose. There may come a time in your future when you are stumped when presented with a choice. Just touch my ring and ask yourself, " What would Audry say?" If it helps you just once, then it did its job.

The letter might help you in those early morning hours, before the sun rises, when you are enjoying some self-induced pity. Dawn, just read it, than give thanks for the time you had with Chet. It will bring back balance to your life.

Enough said about that!

Now for my ashes.

You may think this is a crazy request, but I have thought long and hard about it.

I ask that you take my ashes back to Westside. I was born there, grew up there, and taught there. I think it is only fitting that I end up there. Inside the urn, you will find two bags of ashes. I ask that you take one bag and spread it on the football field, where I was crowned Queen in 1939. I already received permission from the Superintendent for this. Just stop by the office and let him know.

Honey, the second bag goes to a special place. Take the road that goes by the high school one and one-half miles south. You will see a gate that opens into a large hay field on the right side of the road. Remember when I told you the story of Roger and I, and I said I drove out to a hay field, read the letter again, and had a good cry? Well, that is the field, and that's where the other bag should be spread.

I know, you are wondering, why here, it makes no sense!

Dawn, the reason is simple. At that moment, my life changed forever. I would never be someone's Mrs. I had the one love of my life, and even if it was short lived, at least I had him for a while.

I never had another man, wasn't even tempted. I threw myself into teaching, and mentoring young teachers. You, by far, were my best work of art.

So that's why the field is so important. The action you take of spreading my ashes there may result in something else growing in the future. The farmer who owns the land has given his permission to do this. Dawn, it's the Wilson boy who wrote the poem, " Hands". Remember?

Well, that is about it. Maybe, someday, you will give my ring to one of those girls you are helping, maybe on her wedding day.

You know how special you always were to me, like the daughter I never had.

Thank you for all you gave me. My next quest is to find your Mom, Kris, and seek out some pie. Hell, it's got to be real good in Heaven!

Enough said,
Audry

Dawn laid the letter down on the table, wiped her eyes, and took a deep breath. She would do everything Audry asked of her. But she did not want to do it alone. She had gone from a sense of healing to an open wound in one day, and she thought of her father, mother, husband, and best friend. They were all gone, leaving her by herself, with fields of memories.

Dawn felt the need to talk to someone, and after all those months, she opened her desk drawer to find the phone number, and she placed the call.

Chapter 28

He was standing at his kitchen counter, preparing to make a grilled cheese sandwich and a bowl of tomato soup, hoping it would ward off the chill in his bones. Wind chills of 30 below in Lanesboro were not conducive to any outside photoshoot, so he had decided to watch the cold weather from inside.

He picked up the phone on the second ring and said, "Makenzie Photography, this is Brent. How may I help you?" Dawn replied, "You once sent me a letter saying you were a world champion at listening, and I wondered if you still were?"

He recognized her voice instantly, and his heart skipped a beat as he replied, "Well, if this is Dawn Carrington, then, yes, I still hold the title. It is so good to hear your voice. How can I help you?" Dawn began to pour out the story of Audry, from their first meeting to what had just happened today, emotions pouring out as if the river of sadness could not be contained within its own banks. As she spoke and cried, he listened intently, interjecting at one point that he remembered a person named Audry who was a friend of Dawn's mother, and Dawn replied that yes, she was in Burlington the first time that she and Brent had met.

He continued to listen as Dawn spoke of the three girls she had been mentoring, the workshop for writers that would be in six months, and how she had come to grips with Chet's passing. She added, "Some people say, 'I know what you are feeling,' or 'I am sure you will get better,' but Brent, I know exactly what you went through with Sue, so I think you understand." He replied, "I know what you are feeling, I felt the same pain. Would it help if I traveled with you to take care of Audry's ashes? I could be at your place early Friday, and we could drive to Westside together." Dawn added, "If you really mean it, Friday would work for me. I had a lunch date set with Audry, that day. I guess it's only fitting that I be with her as scheduled."

Brent said he could pick Dawn up by 9:00 A.M. if she would e-mail him directions to her home, and she agreed. He ended the call by saying, "Dawn, thank you for calling me, for letting me be a small measure of comfort. I look forward to seeing you on Friday." When he hung up the phone, he was visibly shaking, he had hoped to hear her voice once more, and yes, he thought, "dreams do come true!"

Dawn felt a sense of calm after talking to Brent. She new this rawness of pain from loosing Audry would eventually subside, but it did help to share her burden with someone else.

After sending the e-mail instructions to him, she felt a wave of exhaustion, and climbed back under her covers, falling into a deep sleep.

Chapter 29

Brent spent the rest of the afternoon in the bliss of memories. Just hearing her voice flooded his heart, bringing back to mind the poems he had written for her. The first, *Unexpected,* was given to her three days after they had met. *I'll Never* was from four or five years ago. He had written it after seeing her and her husband at a gallery opening featuring his work.

Now, after all these years, he would have the pure pleasure of spending one day with her. He began to rationalize the opportunity. She had no idea that he was still in love with her, he had kept it to himself. It first happened while he was in mourning for his wife, and then, when he saw Dawn at the Gallery, the feelings had not changed for him, but she was happily married, and it would go against all he believed to "muddy the waters".

Destiny had stepped in, and, if for only one day, he would relish each moment, not counting on anything else, not raising false hope. He was going to be there as one human supporting another in time of need, and that would be enough.

After a quiet supper, he spent the rest of the evening listening to music. The fare consisted of Tony Bennett, James Taylor, and Barbara Streisand. He chuckled to himself and said, "You are such a romantic sap!" But this was music that always calmed and fed his soul.

At 3:12 in the morning, Brent awoke with a poem in his head.

As of late, this had been happening to him more and more, and he knew if he didn't write it down, he would lose it. He was still perplexed on how the words seemed to flow from his heart, but he considered it a blessing from above.

With a fresh brewed cup of coffee in his hand, he moved to his desk, opened his laptop, and began.

One Thousand Times

One Thousand Times
I have seen your face in my mind
Blue eyes tempting me to become lost in love
Surrounded by long lashes that,
With a slow, sultry wink, ignite my inner core
The gentle laugh lines that appear
As you reveal to me your passion for life
For people, for family, for inner self
Framed by a thick mane of hair
That soaks in the sun's blessing
Turning the color into ten shades of gold
Setting off the perfect nose
With just the right amount of upturn
Followed by full, delicious lips, slightly parted
That can become a smile that lights my soul
One thousand times
I have been mesmerized by a glimpse of your neck
As you lift your hair to the top of your head
Bending gently, as if you were a regal swan
I study your shoulders , they are the key to your mood
Covered by a sweater, casual and content
Wrapped in a silk blouse or dress, confidence and awareness
That all others notice
Especially me

One thousand times
I have studied your feminine form
Knowing each firm contour and valley
The magical way it moves
God's perfect structure in gentle motion
That will accept or reject an invitation
To be as one
Over the years I have been tempted
From veiled flirtatious to cheek blushing bawdiness
All were declined, politely
Wanting to save myself for you

One thousand times
I have watched you walk away, into the sunset
Only to return at sunrise
In my mind
To grow together as old age changes our bodies
To grow together as our love becomes richer, fuller
All encompassed
To be held
In that final moment

One thousand times
You were mine
I pray that tonight
Will make one thousand and one

Brent Makenzie

After he read through the poem one last time, his body was asking for sleep, and his last wish before morning darkness would be the day he could see her heart as she read his work.

Chapter 30

Friday morning dawned cold, but still clear. While she waited, nervously, for Brent to arrive, she had taken time to call Sadie to check on the girls. She also explained the situation about Audry, and Sadie decided that the girls should skip the next meeting with Dawn, so she could have some personal time.

She graciously thanked Sadie, and promised to be in touch soon.

Brent had arrived, and after a brief tour of her home, they climbed into his motor home, set the urn carefully between the front seats, and headed out to Westside. After a few minutes of awkward silence, Dawn said, "I really appreciate you helping me. My next favor from you, if I may ask, is that you fill me in on all you have done since your show about the Mississippi River." Brent was thankful for a subject to start a conversation, and he began.

One and a half hours later, as they pulled into Westside, he had told Dawn of all the locations he had shot at, the subjects went from two lane roads to cliff dwellings, abandoned towns in North Dakota, and finding the original pieces of Route 66 that still existed.

When they pulled into the football stadium parking lot, he looked into her eyes, and in a soft, reflective voice, said, "Dawn, it has been a pure pleasure to be able to visit with you about my life, even if the conversation was one-sided. I guess I lead a lonely existence, but that is my choice."

They both noticed a groundskeeper when they exited the RV, and Dawn waved at the man, who came over, saying, "Well, if it isn't Mrs. Carrington. It's good to see you." Dawn, finally remembering his name, introduced him to Brent, "Brent, this is Mike Hobson, a real institution here at Westside High." Brent nodded at him, and Mike said, "I was real sorry to hear about Audry. I had a crush on her for years, but never knew how to start up with her, I guess I'll never know." Dawn told him their plan, and Mike nodded his approval. She and Brent walked onto the field, and went to the home side at the fifty-yard line. In a quiet voice, Dawn said, "This is where the new Homecoming Queen stands each year to accept the crown. Here is where the first ashes must go." She took the first bag out of the urn, carefully cut one of its corners, and began to release the contents. Suddenly, a whirly-wind appeared, and carried some ashes to the top of the bleachers next to the press box, and gently deposited them. Dawn clutched her heart as she watched, realizing that was the exact place where Audry's photo was taken as the first Queen. She said, aloud, as she looked up to the sky, "O.K., I get it.!"

As they walked out, Brent gently put his hand in hers and asked, "Are you all right?" and she smiled back and nodded a yes. He held her hand until they got back in the RV, and Dawn did notice how good it felt to sense another person's touch.

They headed south for two miles to a cross road, so Brent could turn around without going off-road, and came back north to the hay field. After parking along the gravel road, they walked into the hay field with the rest of the ashes.

Dawn withdrew Roger's letter, written in 1952, from her coat, and read it out loud. When she had finished, Brent handed her a tissue, so she could dry her eyes.

As they began to pour out the ashes, they noticed a pick-up truck had stopped by the gate. A tall gentleman stepped out of the drivers side, stood quietly in the gravel road as he took off his seed corn hat, and bowed his head.

When all the ashes had been dispersed by the gentle breeze, he replaced his hat, got back in his truck, and drove down the road, giving a nod to Dawn as he passed.

She looked at Brent, said, "Those Wilsons," and started back to the RV. Brent asked, "What Wilsons?" to which she replied, with a chuckle, "Long story. Someday, when I am up to it, I will tell you."

They drove back past the high school, turned east on Highway 30, and headed towards Ames. Brent had mentioned Hickory Park, and Dawn said she was all in.

The lunch was comforting, as was the company. When they left the restaurant to travel to Dawn's home, she thanked him again for his time and compassion, which he replied," You deserve it." On the twenty-mile drive north, she caught herself sneaking glances at him, noticing he was still an attractive man, the beginnings of gray in his hair adding to the distinguished look.

When they arrived at her home, she asked if he would walk to the grove with her. He accepted, and within a few moments, could sense the importance of that place. Quietly, he said, "I am getting the same feeling here that I sensed at the cliff dwellings just outside Durango, Colorado. There are strong spirits here." And Dawn whispered, "If you only knew the ones who have gone before us."

As they walked back to his RV, she gently took his hand in hers. Before opening his door, she asked, "Would you hold me for just a moment?" and he tenderly wrapped his arms around her, catching a wisp of her scent on her neck, all of his feelings rushing through his veins. He dared not to utter a word, didn't want to break this magic spell. She finally stepped back, lightly touched his face, and said, "It was so good to see you. If you would like, you may call me in the near future." She turned and went into the house, as he watch her every move. His drive back to Lanesboro was filled with a pleasing contentment of the day, and hopes for tomorrow. And, that night became 1,001.

Chapter 31

Winter had passed, and spring had arrived, showing its full glory. Just on the edge of the pine grove, Dawn had found new clusters of Dutchman's Breeches, and three Jack-in- the-Pulpits.
They had never been there before, and to Dawn, it was a sign.

After visiting with Brent on the phone about the girls, she had decided to accept Sadie's proposal. They had met in Jenny's office where the paperwork was signed and notarized. When they finished, Dawn took Sadie's hands in hers and said, "I will do my best when the time comes, but I pray it won't be for years. All three of those girls worship you, and they need you."

And Sadie said, simply, "Thank you."

The girls came to Dawn's house every other Saturday. Their writings had evolved into a beautiful children's story, full of adventure and imagination.

Dawn knew she was biased, so she had asked Sondra about the possibility of *The Written Word* acting as the publisher for the girls. After Sondra read a complete outline, and viewed the images that Meadow had taken, she had placed a call to Dawn, telling her how much she loved the project, that she had been stuck in her office far too long, and wanted to fly out during Easter break to meet the girls.

Dawn cheerfully replied, "That would be perfect! I will reserve a suite at the local B&B in Story City, and we can surprise the girls, together. Oh, by the way, I have been working on a new manuscript since Audry passed, I thought you should know."

Dawn then called Sadie, telling her about the arrangements, and swearing her to secrecy. Sadie was all in, saying that anything that would help the girls grow was O.K. in her book.

Easter break happened to fall on April Fool's Day. The girls had arrived, and Dawn explained that a special guest was coming for lunch. The menu would consist of Iowa beef cheeseburgers prepared on the grill, potato chips, and chocolate malts. When Lark heard that, she chimed in, "This mystery guest must be really important to be granted a malt!"

Sondra arrived, introductions were made, and over a delicious lunch, Sondra explained a brief version of how a book comes to reality. She surprised the girls with a set of story boards her illustrator had worked on, and the girls were thrilled. After lunch, Wren took Dawn aside and whispered, "Thank you for all you have done. I hope you know how much we love you." With a lump in her throat, Dawn replied, "I want you three to realize that anything in life is possible. With a dream comes hard work, but the rewards are a satisfaction you have never felt before. That is the feeling I want you three to achieve."

After lunch, the girls took a walk down to the grove, and Sondra and Dawn enjoyed a cup of coffee on the porch.

Sondra said, "I envy you. To have young people respect you, to have a desire to learn from you, is very special. Half of my life is calming down pissed-off authors, and the other half is juggling all the facets to get a book out the door. Speaking of books, I would love to see the manuscript you have been working on!" Dawn replied, with a sly smile, "Not until it is complete, and up to Carrington standards." Sondra nodded, understanding, saying, " Writers!"

The ladies decided that Sondra would come back in June to show the girls a complete draft, and her trip would coincide with the workshop. Dawn said, "That reminds me, I need to call Chris to see if any of the writers chose to submit poetry."

Sadie swung by to pick up the girls, Sondra drove back to Des Moines to catch her flight, and Dawn, feeling exhausted, headed to the grove with a light blanket and pillow to see if a person could really nap there. The answer was yes.

Chapter 32

After her nap, Dawn left a message for Chris. He finally called her back one week later, and was very apologetic, "I am so sorry, but I didn't receive your message until today. I was out at our winery, by Mt. Hood, and there is no cell coverage there. I was working as a day laborer, getting an insight of how the operation runs, and working with my hands really rejuvenates me. Now, to answer your question, the poetry submissions are coming in at a snail's pace. They are due by May 1st, and Dawn, you know that writers are notorious for waiting till the last minute. So, how have you been?"

Dawn filled him in on the girls' book project, and gave him a few teasers about the manuscript she was working on. Chris replied, "So, the Chet Carrington influence lives on! Dawn, I can't wait to meet you and the girls in person. I will let you know when the poems have been submitted. Have a nice day!"

By the due date, Chris had received nine poems. He spent part of the next three days reading them, laying them down for awhile, then coming back to read them again.

Some of the poems were technically correct, with strong meter and rhyme, but lacked a level of emotion that Chris was looking for. He wrote a note that he would use in a workshop class on poetry: *To me, if I come away from reading a poem and not shed a tear, or looked inside myself, then as a reader, I consider that you have wasted my precious time, time that will never be replaced.*

Satisfied with his quote, he left a message on Dawn's phone, explaining that nine poems were received, but only five met his standard. He would mail them to her, and they would be blind submissions, the author's names were removed. He explained that he wanted her opinion on the work, not the person.

Chris read each of the chosen five one more time, and put them in the mail to Dawn.

Shadow Step

Remember, when you were young
You would chase your shadow
As you took a step, it would, too
The faster you walked, the faster the shadow moved
Always beyond reach
And when you turned around, it vanished from sight
Where are you today, shadow?
In your youth, you would walk with the sun at your back
Casting a long shadow ahead
Now, in maturity, you walk towards the light
No shadow ahead, yet a long one behind
Is the one behind made from deeds, good and bad?
Are all the souls you touched gathered there?
Is your shadow's name " Life?"
As the sun sets lower, your shadow lengthens
Until that moment of last light
After sunset
When it vanishes
At next morning's first light, you are gone
Never to reappear
Will your shadow named "Life"
Survive?
Will someone else take a step
In your shadow?

Sunday Feeling

Freshly laundered and cleansed
Your mind discarding all that happened
The previous week, both good and bad
Washed away by the time you walk into the sanctuary
To find your seat, in your pew
The same spot for decades
So God will notice when He takes attendance
The opening hymn begins to deliver the feeling you desire
Followed by His word
The sermon
The prayers, for those we know, and the one's we don't
Communion at the rail
The body of Christ given for you
The blood of Christ shed for you
You pray
Silently
And listen for an answer
Receive the Benediction
May the Lord make his face shine down on you
Now leaving the church with a full cup of
Fresh, untainted soul
How long does it last? This feeling?
Until you witness
Cruelty, Greed, Unkind Words and Deeds
On Monday

Or, by luck, Wednesday
I pray, Lord
How do I keep this feeling
Until
Next Sunday

Display Window

She is awakened in the middle of a cold,
Blue velvet winter night
By a memory
Pressing her nose to the glass
Of a display window
At Christmas time
On the square
Where all the merchants have displayed
Their finest wares
She has found her wish, a doll house
Two-story Colonial, white with green shutters
Fully furnished
With a miniature couple gazing at each other
In bliss
She felt this was all a ten year old
Wanted
Needed
And desired

On that Christmas morning, under the tree, for her
Barbie doll
Eight track stereo
Nancy Drew mystery book

She was grateful for her gifts

But in secret, she felt crushed
No doll house, no couple in bliss

Emotion of disappointment stayed hidden for decades
Until last week
While passing by the same window
That now framed a coffee shop
Sat that couple
From her doll house
Intimate conversation
His eyes full of love
Her hand seductively resting on his

Emotion, long hidden, became overwhelming
She thought, defiantly
That should be me
I want one night with him
A night that would turn into
A lifetime of tomorrows

Sadly, she recognized disappointment
He belonged to
Another

Porch Swing

At the end of a quarter mile lane
It still stands
Home
Paint peeled, faded by time
Porch swing still hanging
Chains rusted
Floorboards worn by fifty years of shoe soles
Pushing gently
The place where you heard the stories
The Cat in the Hat, Green Eggs and Ham
T'was the Night Before Christmas
For the first time
Snuggled in a long gone Grandma's quilt
Safe and warm

The swing was the place
Late at night
Where you heard your parent's whispers
As they held hands, swinging gently

Your Mother would sit and watch
As you walked up the lane from the school bus
Cookies and cold milk waiting
Her question was always the same
"What did you learn today?"

Your answer never changed, "Nothing!"
She always laughed

The swing
Where you sat with your first date
Tongue tied, palms sweating
Wondering what to say
Knowing she felt the same way

Then, as young lovers
Swinging in the cool night air
Realizing that the number of stars you shared
Equaled your life's possibilities

Later
Your child wrapped in a long gone great Grandma's quilt
Asking that simple, one word question
"Why?"
And each answer you gave was followed by yet another
"Why?"

Finally
The last time you gathered comfort
From that gentle, swinging, motion
Holding tight to the chain
As they all drifted out to their cars and trucks
After the wake

Nodding at you in silence
For you, all that was left
Were
Memories

Portrait

Canvas stretched tight, mounted on an easel
Palette ready
Brushes and knives laid out like surgical instruments
Oils ready to be mixed
To capture the inspiration, to bring the image to life
The life that comes with many layers
From smooth and innocent
To lines, deep and ingrained
A history of living
From youthful wonderment, to mature reality
A trail of scars from life's battles
Interlaced with moments of pure joy
Laugh lines, "Crows Feet", deep, furrowed brow
Blemished skin from weathering all the storms
Eyes with the depth of the past
Looking towards the future
Seeking adornment, acceptance ,and love
Each moment in life
Visible
At this exact place in time
The artist begins mixing color, applying layers
Painting life's light before it expires
The subject will only look like this
Once
Tomorrow will bring changes

From earth shaking to the slightest subtleness of a breath
That will alter the perception of what one sees
Each moment brings more layers of complexity
The final stroke captures what has been
For posterity
Leaving the future to
Imagination

Chapter 33

Dawn retrieved the message from Chris, and made a mental note to be sure and check the mail three or four days from then.

She was looking forward to reading the poetry.

She then placed a call to Brent. Over the past couple months their phone calls had increased from once a week to three times a week. There were five minutes conversations, others lasted past one hour. She felt a calm comfort knowing that they could talk about any subject, differ on opinions, and still respect the other's outlook.

At first, Dawn would have a sense of guilt after talking with Brent. She wondered if it was correct, Chet had been gone almost one year. "Was that permissible in today's society?" she would ask herself.

She would think of Audry, the loss still fresh on the surface, and wonder what her thoughts on the subject would be? She would then laugh, as she imagined Audry's reply, "Hells Bells woman! I thought I taught you better than this. You are a vibrant woman, still on the edge of being attractive, with blood flowing through your veins. You told me yourself he could have had you years ago, but passed because he was in mourning. So, here you are now, with switched positions, and you are concerned about societies outlook on a correct time of mourning? B.S., and I don't mean the degree!"

"Ask yourself one thing, 'How long will I live?' You know damn well there is no right answer to that. So, if you want to have a fulfilled life in your 'Golden' years, take a chance on Brent. Enough said."

Over the next few days, Dawn allowed her thoughts of Brent to run free. In her mind, she compared it to the small boats she would make as a child, attaching a note to her departed father, and letting it find a course on its own in the vastness of the Mississippi River.

She thought of Chet. He was devastated when he lost Michelle. If he hadn't opened his heart to Dawn, where would her life be, today?

Dawn decided, after the workshop was finished, she would invite Brent to her home for a weekend, and just let it progress from there. She also thought, " Is he that interested in me? He has led a solitary life for over twenty years. Maybe he is content with his own, unencumbered lifestyle, being a photographer on the road."

All she would do is issue an invitation, and let destiny work.

She spent the rest of the day reading the poetry that had come in the mail, and ended up going through a box of tissues.

Chapter 34

Brent was doing his own soul searching. He so enjoyed the moments he spent with Dawn on the phone. He was one of the people who believed the art of conversation was in jeopardy of becoming extinct. Texting, e-mail, and all the other social media sites had taken the lead in communication. A one-on-one conversation was more than words. It was emotion, the nuance of a slight change in voice, the rise and fall of pitch and breath. That, he thought, was human reality.

And reality is what he faced now, with his feelings for Dawn. He had purposely been holding back, not wanting to press, to upset her. He, above all people, knew the art of mourning, and each person had their own internal compass leading them from despair to hope.

He knew it was time for him to confess all he felt for her. Two-plus decades of loving someone, without them knowing, wasn't fair to either. The worst case, she would not want to see him again. The best case, she would want to take their relationship to the next level.

Either way, he decided to write her a letter, lay out the truth, and let destiny work.

My dearest Dawn,

Do you remember the man you introduced me to at the football field in Westside? I believe his name was Mike Hobson. He made a statement to us that stuck under my skin for these past months, and I need to address it with you. He said, "I had a crush on Audry for years, but I never knew how to start up with her. Now, I guess I'll never know."

Dawn, here was a common man who voiced his regret as if he never had a choice. Did you notice his eyes? They seemed empty, no happiness, no love. He just settled. He never reached. He never grasped. His existence today is a product of his actions in the past.

I do not want to be another Mike. I want to strive with all I have to lay out my feelings for you, and then, at least I will know that I tried.

Dawn, I fell in love with you by the time we had our third meeting. You didn't encourage it, it wasn't planned, it just happened to me.

Do you remember the poem I gave you on our third date, "Unexpected"? " Years from now, a warm memory, turns into a smile, when I remember you" Well, every day since then, you have been the first thought in my mind in the morning, and the last thought before I fall asleep. In just those few days we were together, I memorized everything about you, your face, your body, your walk, your voice, the look in your eyes. I have been able to recall all of that a thousand times over the years.

Dawn, I loved you then, but the timing was not right. I love you today, deeper than before. Life experience will do that. I am sure you loved Chet more with each year you two had together.

When you called me in January, it was as if a prayer had been answered. I couldn't wait to see you again. When I was at your home, I watched you walk out of the office, you wore a brown sweater and jeans, and the sun gave a perfect back-light to you, surrounding you with a glow. I actually felt my heart skip, and I had to draw a quick breath. That's how beautiful you seem to me. And, it's not just the outside beauty that I love, it is also what is inside you.

The way you are mentoring those three girls is amazing. You are giving back, building their confidence, imploring them to use imagination, teaching them the fact that it is O.K. to dream. All of that makes me love you more.

Dawn, I want to make love with you, I want to take long walks with you, I want to grow old with you, I want to look in those deep pools of blue and see your love for me.

There it is. Please read this more than once, and if and when you would like to talk, call me. I will give you your space until I hear from you.

All my love,
Brent

Chapter 35

Two days later, Dawn walked to the end of her driveway to get her mail. She noticed that in among all the junk mail was an envelope from Makenzie Photography. Her initial thought was, "I bet this is an invitation to his next show, I think in Mason City". When she got back inside, she poured a fresh cup of coffee, then sat at the kitchen table and opened his letter.

After reading it the first time, she was stunned. She had never seen the signs that would have given her an insight to Brent's feelings. The second time through caused tears. Brent was right about his observations of Mr. Hobson. Dawn had worked beside him for sixteen years, and he always seemed lonely. If he had just said something to Audry, his life might have been fuller. Dawn's memory opened up, and she recalled that on more than one occasion, Audry had made some positive comments about Mike Hobson, like, "Always nice, very polite, rather shy." Dawn remembered an old adage, "Two ships that passed in the night"

After the third reading, she decided to call Brent. He picked up on the second ring, and Dawn began, " I just read your letter three times. Please just listen. Thank you for writing, thank you for telling me all that you felt. One of the things that attracted me to you at those first meetings was your honesty. Now, I need to admit some things to you. I have been thinking a lot about you since we went to Westside. I stole more than one look at you while you were driving, wondering what it would be like, you and I together. I didn't approach you, I felt it was still too early after Chet's passing. I do have feelings for you, so I have a suggestion.

This upcoming writer's workshop is going to get all of my attention. When it is finished, I will need a week to revive myself. After that, I would very much like you to spend a weekend with me here at the house. No pressure, just two people enjoying each other. Brent, is that acceptable to you?"

He let out a long sigh, and in a choked up voice, replied, "It would be an honor to spend time with you, nothing would make me happier." Dawn, smiling, replied, "It is an official date! I will call you after I am recouped, and we will pick a weekend that works. Brent, until then, I will be thinking of you. Bye for now!"

As he hung up his phone, he bowed his head and whispered, "Thank you, Lord."

Chapter 36

In Portland, Chris was busy pulling all aspects of what he wanted to accomplish at the workshop together. He was still checking the mail daily, hoping for a few more poetry submissions. This day's mail provided just one piece, a hand-addressed envelope from his mother, Katherine. He was used to receiving trust reports from her, but they always came by messenger.

As he slit open the letter, he could see it was written by hand. He thought, "This must be a life-changing event!" After taking a bottle of sparkling water from his wine cooler, he went out to the terrace to sit at the bistro table. He took a long, cool drink, and began to read:

To my dearest Christopher,

I hope you know that you are, and have always been, the most important person in my life. Everything I have done since the day I first held you was to benefit you, to give you financial freedom so you could become a dream catcher. Even as a young child, you seemed to have an old soul, and you were always fascinated by words, and how those words could convey emotion. You have turned out to be an amazing writer, the national awards you have received solidify that, and my heart overflows with pride.

Son, what you are about to read is true, the facts about how you came to be. When you have finished reading this, I ask that you not judge me. I believe only God has that right. You may wonder, "Why now?" As you know, I turned 60 this year, and I want to sweep the floor clean, so there will be no more unanswered questions.

It is 1987, I had just turned 35, and was perched on top of the financial mountain. All the possessions a person wanted, I had. The penthouse that we lived in was mine, free and clear, along with the rest of the nine stories in the building below us. Each year I had a new Mercedes Benz. Behind my back, my male counterparts, my competitors in business, nicknamed me "Ice Queen". I took them all on, and beat them at their own game.

On paper, I had it all. In my personal life, I had one goal left, and that was to have a child. I approached it as a business venture. Having a relationship, dating, having to please someone, none of that appealed to me. I set out to find a man to father my child, no, to create a child. There would be no "Fathering" in the equation.

In the fall of that year, I purchased a suite at the Benson Hotel downtown. It was close to all the places where high-end events were held. I would attend these events to find the man I needed.

On December 10, 1987, I went to an opening at the Littman-White Gallery at PSU. A photographer from Iowa was exhibiting fine art black and white prints consisting of old buildings and landscapes. The show was called, "Rural Iowa Ruins".

Chris, the image that hangs in my library came from that show. The title is, "All That Remains", and the photographer told me he had taken the image in Morrill Hall at Iowa State University.

As I was looking at that image, a low, soft voice behind me said, "Black and white photography brings out the raw emotion of the subject, don't you agree?"

I turned around and saw the man I was searching for. Tall, wavy blond hair that came down past his shirt collar, blue eyes that looked much older than him, good shape, neat dresser. I gently put my arm through his, and we walked slowly around the exhibit, critiquing each image.

He was very good at small talk, and I found out he was in town for three days on business. After viewing all the images, I said, "Not to appear bold, but, since you are not from here, I would like to take you to dinner. Morton's Steakhouse is just a few blocks down, and I am just craving a medium-rare Filet Mignon. Would you please consider joining me?" He replied, "That is a gracious offer, and I accept." We both walked under one umbrella, and before he could ask, I put my arm around him and said, "It's December in Portland, you can bank on it raining constantly!" We had a great dinner with three glasses of a fine merlot, each.

I asked where he was staying, and he replied, "The Benson". I smiled and replied, "What a small world, I live at the Benson. Shall we?"

I nodded at the maître d, and he knew to put the bill on my account.

We walked the few blocks to the hotel, and I invited him up for coffee. He was hesitant, so I kissed him gently on the lips, and whispered, "No strings attached." While the coffee was brewing, I removed his tie and sport coat, and asked him to get comfortable while I changed. When I came back, he was sitting at the kitchen table, so we had coffee there. I could tell that he wanted to talk, that some pain had been inside him for a very long time, and I offered to listen.

He explained that two years earlier, his wife of fifteen years had died of cancer, and he had not been on a date or been with a woman since then. He firmly said he was not ready for any relationship.

I got up from my chair, walked around to him, kissed him full on the lips, looked into his eyes, took his hand, and I said, "I do not want any relationship, I do not want any ties that bind. I just want you in my bed, tonight."

Chris, I will spare you the details. He and I were together for three days and nights. The only time he left my suite was to attend an event at Powells Book Store. They had twenty authors in for a mass book signing, and he was one of them.

We said goodbye to each other on the morning of December 13th, and we never saw or talked to each other again. Remember, no strings.

Two months later, I was having morning sickness, and nine months and one week after he left, you were born on September 20th, 1988.

Son, if I had to do it all over again, I would not change a thing. I believe I helped him come to grips with his grief, and I got you, my precious son.

So, now you know all the facts, accept one.

Your father's name was Chester T. Carrington, the best selling author.

With a Mother's love,
Katherine

Chapter 37

Chris was in a state of shock. He felt anger and deceit towards his mother, a sense of loss towards his father. He thought, "How could she hold this from me for all these years? Didn't she consider my right to know my father? And what about Chet? He never knew he had a son, a son who was a writer. If I had known, I never would have written *Missed.* My life would have been completely different. What am I suppose to do with this? How do I find my way through it?"

And then, another thought, "What about Dawn Carrington? Does she need to know? Would she want to know?"

Chris began the process of decision making, picking out different scenarios, defining the probability of damage and pain, the need to know verses protection from the truth, and calculating the final result. By morning, he had made a decision and set a lunch appointment with his mother. She was actually surprised that he had called, and she cleared her schedule for the rest of the day.

Chris knocked on his mother's door, and she opened it, stepping back with a tentative look on her face, a look that Chris had never seen. He closed the door behind him and walked to her, wrapping her in his arms. He said, softly, "I love you, I appreciate you, and I thank you for the truth. I can't imagine what it must have been like to keep a secret like that for all these years. Let's sit down, and I will tell you what I have decided."

They moved to the dining room table where sandwiches and chips were laid out, along with a crystal pitcher of iced tea with lemon. Chris poured a glass, and began, "My main concern now is Dawn, Chet's widow. She is not responsible for any of this, yet she could end up being hurt by the truth. I will not bring up the subject unless she asks. And why would she ask? Mother, when was the last time you looked at the dust jacket on Chet's first book?"

Katherine did not respond, so Chris walked down the hall to the library, retrieved the book, and brought it back to the table. He continued, "Chet was the same age that I am now when this book was published. Does his picture resemble anyone you know?"

There was nothing but silence in the room. Finally, Katherine, in a hushed voice, responded, "You are a carbon copy of your father. Every line on your face, your eyes, your hair, your nose, even your voice, are his. The way you think, the way you write, the way you treat others, all of that came from him. When Dawn sees you for the first time, she will know."

Chris asks her, "Why does this book look so worn?"

With tears streaming down her face, Katherine whispers, "I have held that book a thousand times, just to touch his picture, read his words, and to memorize his inscription to me in the front:
To Kat, Wishing you a fulfilled life. From Chet."

"Son, people say you can fall in love at first sight. For me, it took three days, but then he was gone, gone forever. My damn pride would not allow me to call him, to find him, to tell him he was needed. My shear stupidity of thinking that I could not show weakness and vulnerability cost me the chance to grow old with him. It cost you, son, the chance to say, 'Dad'".

She took the book in both hands, sobbing as she cried out, "God, I beg your forgiveness."

Chris held her until calm came over her, and when he started toward the door, she asked, "Honey, why weren't you mad at me?" And he replied, "Mother, you know I never keep score."

Chapter 38

The countdown had started. There were thirty days left until the opening session of the workshop, and Dawn was checking on all the details. Her list included: airline flights, rooms, meals, transportation, entertainment, and supplies.

She had received a call from Sondra that morning about an idea. She told Dawn, "I have been researching old photos of Chet on the Internet, it is amazing what you can find online. With your permission, I want to produce a photomontage of his life to present to the attendees. I found his graduation picture from the 1974 ISU "Bomb", and one of Michelle, who was listed as an Alpha Xi Delta trainer. I also found pictures of him at book signing events in New York, Chicago, Minneapolis, Denver, and Portland. The two from Portland were in the *OREGONIAN DAILY* files. The first one is a shot that was taken at an art opening, dated December 10, 1987, and he is standing with some black and white prints behind him, with a woman on his arm. The caption reads, "Portland's Elite Support the Littman-White Gallery", and the article says, "The movers and shakers of Portland's art scene turned out in force last night for an opening of black and white fine art images called, *"Rural Iowa Ruins"*. In attendance was Katherine Cody, a Portland business icon, and best selling author, Chet Carrington, pictured above."

The other one was from a book signing at Powell's Book Store, taken the following day. It shows Chet signing a book for Katherine. Dawn, can you believe the irony in this? Here is Chet with Katherine, and twenty-five years later, her son, Chris, is the first instructor for the Chet Carrington Writer's Workshop. How is that for a small world!!!

Anyway, I will e-mail all these images on a pdf to you, along with a headshot of Chris and his bio. Please select the ones you want, and let me know tomorrow, so I can schedule a print run.

Also, I think the girls are going to be elated when they see the new storyboards my staff completed for their book. Dawn, bye for now."

With all the planning, Dawn had neglected to call Chris to discuss the poetry submissions. She reached him later in the day, and told him that the five poems he sent really moved her, that he owed her a new box of tissues, and that Sondra had just sent her old photos, that two of them were of Chet and his mother. She continued, "Both Sondra and I mentioned how ironic it was to see them together. All of your arrangements have been made, your rental car will be at the airport, and we can't wait to see you on June 13th. Any questions?"

Chris replied, "I would like a copy of those pictures. Would you please do that for me?" Dawn answered, "They will be here when you arrive. Have a nice day!"

After Chris hung up his phone, he said, out loud, "She will figure it out before I arrive."

Dawn's next call was to Sadie, to check on the girl's schedules.

Sadie said the girls were tied up with school year-end activities and softball games, but June 13th would work out for them to come and spend the day. Dawn replied, "That is the day that Sondra arrives, so that will work out fine. I thought I would have the girls give her a tour of the sculptures that would be featured in the book." Sadie agreed, so that was set.

After a light supper, Dawn poured a glass of merlot and sat at the kitchen table to review the photos that Sondra had sent. She started with the graduation photos of Chet and Michelle and thought, "They look so young and innocent, free of life's tarnish and trouble, and you can see love in their eyes.

She looked up at the portrait of her and Chet that she had brought back from the cabin at Christmas, and thought, "Dealing with the grief of loosing Michelle, and the five years he spent in his 'wilderness of life' had taken its toll. The lines on his face were deeper, his hair had gone from blonde to gray, but his eyes were still intense."

The images from his book signings all had one thing in common. He was "Mr. Social". The way he smiled at people, the way he would listen to them, as if they were the only two people in the room.

Dawn then studied the photo of Chet and Katherine at the Gallery, and thought, "A women knows when another woman has designs on her man, and it looks like Katherine is trying to close the deal."

She then opened the packet about Chris. His bio was: Born September 20, 1988, raised by a single mother, attended private school, graduated early from PSU, award-winning author and poet, runs his

own non-profit charitable foundation, and cooks at the homeless shelter once a month.
Dawn thought, "Katherine must be very proud of her son, and to think she raised him being a single parent and business woman. Very impressive!"

She then pulled out an 8x10 glossy head shot of Chris from the packet, and her heart skipped a beat. Rising from the table, she carries the shot over to the portrait on the wall and compares Chet to Chris. They are identical in every way except the hair. Chet's was gray, while Chris was blonde. Dawn sits back down at the table and checks the bio again. Date of birth *9/20/1988.*
She then looks at the date of the Gallery photo: *12/10/1987.*

The math was easy. Nine months and ten days.

Dawn refills her wine glass and walks out to the screen porch to sit at the bistro table. A wave of sadness washes over her. She thinks, "My God, he had a son, and never knew it. How could Katherine not tell him. Why would she keep Chris from his father? Does Chris know?"

The second glass of wine had done the job. Dawn was more relaxed now, and she thought of a phrase she had written in a poem that she turned into a song, *With saving grace, you found me, destiny arrived, to bring joy to us.*

And then she whispered, "Destiny will arrive here on June 13th."

Chapter 39

Sunrise. June 13th. Clear blue sky. There had been a gentle light rain overnight, and Dawn could smell the fresh pine scent that the breeze waffed over the yard from the grove. She was enjoying her coffee on the porch, cherishing the quiet of early morning, knowing that before this day ended, it would be a three-ring circus, with her as ringmaster.

All the workshop preparation was complete, and by the time it was over, she knew someone's life would be changed. Chet used to say, "If each book I write can influence or change one person's life, then I have done my job."

Dawn heard the crunch of gravel under car tires, and knew that Sadie was there with the girls. They flew from the car, Sadie waved goodbye, and the three mobbed her with hugs and kisses. They all started at once talking about what they had been doing. Dawn laughed and said, "Pick a number between one and twenty." Lark won, Meadow was second, and Wren was last.

Lark began, "I got straight A's on my report card, won the perfect attendance award, and Bobby Douglas tried to kiss me on the last day of school, and I kicked him good, in the shins!"

Dawn doubled over with laughter, then said, "Meadow, can you top that?" She replied, "I believe I can. I, too, received straight A's, the image I took of the Petersen sculpture, *Conversations,* won 1st prize in the school photo contest, and on the last day of school, I allowed Shane McDonough to kiss me on the cheek!"

Dawn looked at Wren and said, "O.K. What do you have that will top that?" Wren began, "Straight A's, six over-the fence home runs in ten-at-bats, my essay entitled *Why I Love Small Town Life* won the writing contest, which came with a $100 gift certificate good at any store in Story City, and when Jerry Johnson tried to ask me to go to the movies on Saturday, I gave him my 'Look', and he walked away like a whipped pup."

Dawn was starting to tell the girls how proud she was of them when a delivery van pulled in, and the driver came over to Dawn with a beautiful bouquet of one dozen yellow roses. She thanked him, and opened the card. It read, *With Anticipation, Brent*. The girls all noticed Dawn's face had gotten red, and before they could ask, Dawn said, "From a friend", and they all responded, in unison, "Whatever!"

No sooner than the van leaving, Sondra pulled into the driveway, and the girls went to greet her. They all helped Sondra carry in big portfolio cases and easels. Everyone grabbed a glass of iced tea, and the presentation began. Sondra explained, "Here is the cover, the title is *The Petersen Sculptures Midnight Escape*." There was a drawing of the Gentle Doctor walking his dog next to the Campanile. Underneath the image, it read, "By Wren, Meadow, and Lark Russell". All the girls let out a cheer when they saw their names. The next poster showed Library Boy and Girl walking, hand-in-hand, on Central Campus, and the next portrayed the students from Conversations walking towards State Gym, with the Dreamer left behind. They continued to look at the posters, and all were pleased.

Sondra said, "This will go to press in July, and will be ready to sell before school starts. Thank you, all, for letting me be a part of this experience. Girls, I need you to give me a guided tour of the real sculptures, and I hope you know a good place to eat."

Lark leaned over, and whispered in Sondra's ear, "If you need a great chocolate malt, I know a place!"

They were out the door in minutes, and Dawn was left with the luxury of quiet and her thoughts of how the girls had blossomed, the book was a great opportunity for them.

She blushed as she gazed at her yellow roses. She, too, was looking forward in anticipation, more than she had thought.

And in seven hours, Chris would arrive.

The all girl crew returned at 4:00 P.M., just as Sadie was pulling in. The three girls still had plenty of energy, but Sondra looked very tired. After the girls left, Sondra commented, "Whatever you are giving those three to eat and drink, I want the recipe. Their positive energy is unbelievable! I am headed to the B&B for a hot bath and a bottle of wine. I will touch base with you mid-morning tomorrow."

When Sondra left, Dawn checked the clock and made a mental note, "One hour left."

She made a fresh pot of coffee, filled her cup, and headed for the porch.

Finally, she heard a car door close, and she went to open the front door to greet him, "Chris, I am Dawn. It is so nice to meet you. Please come in. Are you hungry?" He replied, "No thank you, I grabbed a sandwich in Des Moines before I drove here. I would drink coffee, if it's not a bother." Dawn said, "Certainly," and invited him to sit at the table. His eyes became fixed on the portrait of Chet and Dawn, and after a few minutes of silence, Dawn reached across the table and took his hands in hers, and quietly asked, " How long have you known?"

In a soft, quivering voice, he answered, "My mother told me just three weeks ago. She mailed me a letter that explained everything. I brought it with me in case you wanted to read it."

Quietly, Dawn replied, "There is no need for that. You noticed the portrait. You are the complete image of him. Here are the pictures I said I would copy. The first one is at a Gallery opening on December 10th, 1987." Chris replied, "That is the first time that they met, at that opening." Dawn continued, "The second picture was taken the next day at a book signing." Chris added, "My mother still has that book, He signed it: *To Kat, Wishing you a fulfilled life, From Chet.*

Dawn, I am so sorry about this. She never tried to contact him, she wanted to keep me all to herself, like her other possessions. Then, out of the blue, you extend to me a great opportunity. I am so thankful for you, without your invitation, I would never have heard the truth. Destiny brought us together."

Dawn looked at him and said, "I want to officially welcome you into your father's house." She then placed a small box on the table in front of him, and said, "Please open it." As he looked inside, she continued, "Your father commissioned those cuff links and matching ring years ago. Whenever he dressed up, those were on him. I know he would want you to have them, please wear them in his honor." Chris was overwhelmed with emotion as tears flowed freely down his face. He replied, "I will honor him with everything I will do for the rest of my life. Thank you from the bottom of my heart and soul. For the first time in my life, I am whole."

Silence overcame them. After a long while, Dawn said, "Why not refill your coffee cup and come outside with me." He did, and Dawn walked him to the office. When they entered, she explained, "This is where your father wrote. All those binders on the shelves contain the original manuscripts of every book and poem he had ever written, including one he never published. He said, "I have spent my entire adult life writing for others. I am writing this for me." No one has read it, not even me. Chris, if you want to know your father, these binders are where you should start. And I think it is only fitting that you be the first person to read this one." She gently handed him the only red binder on the shelf and said, "Please sit here at his desk, feel what he felt. I am going to get a drink and take a walk. Take your time, son, you have the rest of your life to learn about your Dad." With that, she kissed the top of his head and left the office.

With hesitant, shaking hands, Chris opened the binder and turned to the start of the first chapter:

Portland Intrigue

By

Chester T. Carrington

Copyright 1988

Chapter one

Rain. Cold. The kind of cold that sinks into every muscle and bone in your body. Day after day, after day, until it sinks into your soul.

He had wandered through the wilderness of life for the past two years. There were meaningless stops in New York, Boston, Chicago, Des Moines, Salt Lake, Seattle, and now, Portland.

His greatest challenge?

A question: Am I running from grief? Am I running from the pain of loss? Am I running from the fear of my own mortality?

Or is it that I am running towards an unattainable goal, to feel young, to feel needed, to be desired by someone.

Could it be the simple, single quest to make a difference in some person's life for a single moment in time?

Time.

Measured by seconds, minutes, hours, days, weeks, years, than decades. Why not measure time by how long a smile can last, how long a simple compliment can make a person's day better.

Can time be measured by love? How long until you see her soul in the depths of her eyes. The measure of anticipation until you can feel the warmth of her body. The number of times you think of her in a day. When will she be taken away?

Are life and love and loss interchangeable in a measure of Time?

Chapter 40

While Chris was reading in the office, Dawn had gone back into the house to pour a glass of wine. She went back outside and noticed a gentle breeze coming from the north. Out of habit, or for the need of comfort, she headed for the pines. She could hear the faint whispers from the grove as the wind gently caressed the boughs.

She chose to sit in his chair tonight, just to be that much closer to him. She wanted to feel his arms around her, to reassure her that all things ahead of her, things she had yet to see, would work out.

Dawn took a long drink of her wine and turned her face towards the sky. Out loud, she said, "Lover, you have a wonderful son!"

And as clear as fine crystal, with that unmistakable voice, Chet answered, "I know my love, I can see from Heaven."